KILLIAN

A DARK MAFIA ROMANCE

NATASHA KNIGHT

Copyright © 2017 by Natasha Knight

All rights reserved.

No part of this book may be reproduced in any form or by any electronic or mechanical means, including information storage and retrieval systems, without written permission from the author, except for the use of brief quotations in a book review.

Killian: a Dark Mafia Romance was originally published with the title Captive Beauty. No change has been made to the text. Only the title has been updated.

ABOUT THIS BOOK

Killian: a Dark Mafia Romance was originally published as Captive Beauty.

Cilla

The Beast had Belle.
Killian Black has me.

How I got here doesn't matter, even though he says it does. Says it was my choice. He doesn't get it, though. It wasn't ever a choice for me.

And now, he's changing the rules.

The agreement was one month. For thirty days, I'd be his. He's no longer satisfied with my body alone, though. He wants my soul, too. Wants every part of me. And even though I can pretend I'm safe when I lie beneath him, this man does something to me. Something wicked.

A thing that will break me.

Killian

Cilla made the choice. She offered the deal. I just took her up on it. So what if I changed the rules half-way in? I'm not apologizing for it.

See, Cilla and me, we're the same. She's dark. As dark as me. Something happened to her. Something bad. It damaged her.

But it's not a hero she seeks. It's an avenging angel. A dark knight. That, I can do. I'll slay her dragons, but it'll cost her, because in return, I want everything. And I'll take it.

She's mine.

PROLOGUE 1
CILLA

He's watching me. I know he is. He has cameras everywhere. Why wouldn't he have one here? In this, the "special" room? He told me he likes to keep an eye on his things. And that's what I am. A thing. A possession.

His.

Fucking his.

And today I fucked up.

Today he'll take it out of my skin.

I shudder with the thought. With the knowledge of what I know is coming.

I'll fight him. I wonder if he expects me to. Wants me to, even. All I know is I can't submit to him. I can't let him break me.

But I am breaking. Little by little.

I wonder if that's why he took me.

This is a game to him. My life is a game.

I hug my knees to myself. This room is so cold, unlike the others.

I pull the blanket up around me, as much for the cold as

for protection. It's not like I can hide my fear. He knows. He knows the real truth. Knows everything now.

My dress is torn and I'm barefoot. He took my shoes away when he put me here. I guess the heels could be used as a weapon. As if I could somehow manage to overpower him.

I try to swallow but the lump in my throat makes it impossible. I'm scared and I hate it. I don't want to admit it. Not even to myself.

Tears wet my eyes but before they have a chance to fall, I cover them with my hands and rub them away. I don't want him to see my weakness. He gets off on it.

I did this. I pushed him. And I can survive this. I fucking have to.

It's when I'm giving myself that ridiculous pep talk that I hear his footfalls in the hallway. Hear his voice, muffled so I can't make out what he says. Probably dismissing Hugo, his fucking henchman. Like he needs one.

Every hair on my body stands on end when he slides the key into the lock. When he turns it. And when he pushes the door open, it takes all I have not to crumple. Not to cave.

It takes all I have to stand and ready myself for battle against this beast of a man.

PROLOGUE 2

KILL

She claims I took her, but that's not the whole truth.

I gave her a choice. She made it.

Someone needed to be punished. It didn't need to be her. She chose this. Chose to be here.

Well, okay, not right here. Not like this. Standing against the far wall, her pretty, jade eyes wide with fear, the delicate skin around them pink from tears.

She's scared.

And she should be.

She knows what's coming.

I warned her and she fucked up.

I take her in, pretty in pink. Pretty Priscilla. Even with her hair a mess. Her mascara a black smear across her face. Her dress ruined. She's scared shitless, but she's defiant. I like that about her. Like her fire.

It makes my dick hard.

I close the door but don't bother locking it. No need. She's not walking out of here tonight. I'll be carrying her when I'm through.

When I take a step, she makes a sound, something like a

frightened little rabbit would make if they could make sound. Her hands are flat against the wall behind her. It's like she's trying to melt into it.

"I guess we were always going to end up here," I say.

She has no response apart from the sudden trembling of her body. She wraps her arms around herself. I can even hear her teeth chatter. She's too proud to beg though. Beg me for mercy. I respect her for that. But I do like the idea of her on her knees at my feet, clinging to me, pleading with me to spare her this one thing.

I slide off my suit jacket and hang it over the back of the chair. I watch her reflection in the mirror as I take off one cuff link, then the other, and set them both on the table. I'm rolling up my sleeves when I return my attention to her. Her eyes slide to my forearms. My hands.

"I know, Cilla," I say.

She looks up at me.

"I know everything."

1

CILLA

Six Weeks Earlier

I'm not paying attention when I step off the elevator on the sixth floor of my brother, Jones's, apartment building. My phone just ran out of charge and I'm digging in my bag for the battery pack. The scent of curry coming from 605 is as familiar as the sound of the television playing too loud from 602, and the baby crying in 601.

Jones and I have a standing dinner date the first Wednesday of every month. Apart from that night, unless he needs something, we don't see each other. I left him a voicemail earlier to meet me in the lobby, but he wasn't there so I had to come up to get him. At least the rain had let up when I'd made the dash into the entrance, but from the sound of water pelting the window at the end of the hallway, it's picked up again.

When I reach his door, I hear the sound of talking. I don't recognize the voice, but it's deep and scratchy, like a man who has been smoking for a long time. I wonder if Jones forgot about our dinner and, before the warning in my head registers, I knock on his door and call out his name, making some comment about how he'd better not stand me up.

But my voice trails off at the end of my own sentence. That's when I know something isn't right.

"Jones?" I ask a little more quietly as I lay my hand flat against the damaged wood.

The door opens a crack.

"Oh, there you are," I start, relieved. But then I see his face. The look in his eyes. There's a bruise forming on his right cheekbone and his lip is cut. I tilt my head trying to process. "What—"

Run.

He mouths that single word as a hand closes around the door, pulling it wide. A hulking man appears behind him, grabs me by the arm and hauls me inside. He thrusts my back against the wall and clamps his hand over my mouth.

"Fuck. Cilla. I'm sorry, I'm so—" But Jones doesn't have a chance to finish his sentence because one of the two men in his apartment knocks the butt of a gun across his temple and Jones crumples to the floor.

I think I scream, but the sound is muffled by the big, meaty hand covering my mouth.

The man who knocked my brother out looks down at him, shakes his head once before turning his gaze to me. I cower, realizing then that I'm clawing uselessly at the arm of the one holding me to the wall.

"Wrong place, wrong time, honey," he says, and the next thing I feel is a sharp pain at the back of my head. Lights explode in my vision before I feel myself slide down the wall and fall over, my eyes closing.

2

KILL

"What the fuck is this?" I'm sitting behind my desk watching the two figures on the monitor. They're passed out, lying on the floor in the basement, hands bound behind their backs. The girl's eyes are covered with a blindfold.

Hugo, the man in charge of the clowns who fucked up tonight, is shaking his head, watching the same monitor. "She walked in on them. Saw their faces. They got scared."

I look at him, tilt my head to the side. "They got scared? What is this, fucking amateur night?" Hugo opens his mouth to answer but I put my hand up to stop him. "Never mind. Did you recover the bag?"

"Yes, sir."

"Well, that's something." I turn back to the screen. "Who is she?" It's only supposed to be that idiot Jones down there.

Hugo opens her wallet and hands me a driver's license. Priscilla Hawking. Jones Hawking's sister. I check her birth date. Twenty-four. She's his kid sister.

I peer at the face smiling at me from the license then back at the screen. She's passed out, and somewhere in transit, must have lost one of her shoes. She's still got her coat on but it's unbuttoned and her skirt's ridden up to expose one slender thigh.

Jones's body shifts a little. He's waking up. I watch as he slowly blinks his eyes open and turns his head a little, surveying the ceiling. An instant later, he shoots upright. I smile. He knows where he is. Why he's there. But then he sees his baby sister there, still passed out on the floor, and he starts crying like a fucking baby himself.

"Should I head down?" Hugo asks.

I almost forgot about him. "No. Give him a minute to appreciate his circumstances." Because tonight, Jones is going to learn a valuable lesson.

I get to my feet. Hugo follows. I unzip the duffel bag my men retrieved and take a rough inventory of its contents. "All here?" I ask Hugo without looking at him.

"Looks to be."

I'm fingering the slit in one of the bricks. "Tampered with."

"He probably took a few hits but we got him when he arranged the sale."

That's how we found out it was Jones who'd stolen the bag. He tried to sell my coke back to one of my own men. Fucking idiot.

But Jones's little stunt comes as a good lesson for me too. It reminds me that just because people fear you, doesn't mean they'll keep their sticky fingers out of your shit.

Tonight, I'll make an example. Remind everyone what happens when you get greedy enough to steal from Killian Black.

I zip the duffel and glance again at the monitor. The girl creates a complication.

"Let's go."

Hugo follows me into the elevator and we ride it down to the main floor. The doors slide open and we step out into the nearly empty room. A girl is dancing on one of the stages and the manager sits watching her. She must be auditioning. I look over at her. Pretty, young, good looking, with a nice set of tits and a tight ass. She needs a little work in the dance department though.

Hugo and I head to the door leading to the staircase where two men stand sentry. They open the door when they see us approach and Hugo follows me down. For as luxurious as things are above ground, they're that primitive below. But the basement, it's not anywhere anyone wants to be.

My steps echo off the walls and the guard standing outside the door straightens.

"Open it," I tell him.

He does. The two inside still instantly, both turning toward us, the girl blind from the cloth covering her eyes. She may have seen the faces of the idiots who kidnapped her, but she hasn't seen me. Doesn't know who I am unless her asshole brother told her.

I enter with Hugo close behind me. He closes the door.

Jones is blubbering, fucking crying again, his words are coming out so fast, I can't make sense of them.

"Shut the fuck up." It's Hugo and he's moved to stand behind the kneeling man. He presses the barrel of a gun to the back of Jones's head.

Jones quiets but for the fucking sniffling. "Jones, don't be a pussy," I say, leaning against the wall, my eyes on the girl. She's quiet, hasn't said a word, but her head snaps in the direction of my voice the moment she hears it. She's on her knees too, but I'm guessing it's because her balance is off with the blindfold and her hands being bound behind her back. I know she's pretty from her driver's license picture, but in person, even with the blindfold on, she's striking, with high cheekbones and plump lips I'm not sure she realizes she's biting.

"Did you tell her what you did?" I ask Jones, not taking my eyes off the girl.

"I didn't do anything. I was just...I found...I accidentally—"

Hugo mutters something and smacks him on the side of the head. It's not a hard smack but Jones shuts up.

"You accidentally found a duffel bag full of coke?"

"Y...yes, sir."

"And then what?" I ask.

"I...I was going to bring it back."

"Do I look like a fucking idiot?"

"Please don't hurt me! Please. I made a mistake. I—"

"Please don't hurt *you*? What about your sister here? Should I hurt *her* instead?" Fucking coward piece of shit.

Jones shakes his head. "It's all there. I was going to give it back."

"Really? After you made arrangements for a sale?"

He takes in a deep breath, realizing I know.

I step toward him. "I have eyes and ears everywhere, understand, fool?"

"Yes, sir."

"My brother made a mistake," the girl suddenly says. "He's not a fool."

Her comment makes me chuckle, but she's not making a joke. Her voice is soft and I know she's trying to act like she's calm, but I can see the pulse at her neck pounding.

"No? Because all evidence points to the contrary."

She's quiet, perhaps thinking how to reply. "Please don't hurt him."

That strikes me. Please don't hurt *him*. Not please don't hurt *us*.

"Should I let him walk out of here scot-free?"

She swallows, exhales a breath. She knows I won't do that.

"Just..." She's shaking her head and tears have wet the blindfold and her cheeks. "I'm sorry."

Her apologizing makes me hate Jones even more. "Help her stand."

Hugo takes her arm and raises her to her feet. She stands on the foot with the shoe, then shifts to the one without it. I step toward her and even though she can't see me, I know she feels the shift because she backs up and stiffens, her face turning upward, searching for me.

"Priscilla Hawking," I say, trying out her name. I want her to know I know exactly who she is.

She visibly shudders.

I move closer, then to her side, slowly behind her, eyeing the ropes that have cut into the skin of her wrists. I lean in and inhale a subtle scent of perfume beneath the acrid one of fear.

"Are you scared?"

She goes rigid. I know she can feel my breath on her neck.

"Answer my question."

"Yes." It's a squeak.

I walk around her, resume my position facing her. "At least one of you is honest. But what kind of message would I be sending if I let Jones walk out of here? If I don't punish him?"

She drops her head, wipes her nose on her shoulder.

"It wouldn't be good for business," I say.

"What are you going to do, then?" she asks, her jaw set when she turns her face up.

"Break a leg. Maybe two." I shrug my shoulder as Jones starts blabbering some nonsense. I realize he's probably stoned.

"I can pay you." Her voice breaks and she can't hide the fact that she's crying now.

I step to her, reach out to touch a tear with my thumb. She gasps.

"This isn't about money, sweetheart."

"Please don't—"

"Shh, Priscilla." I turn to Jones. "Get up."

She obviously thinks I'm going to break his legs right here, right now, because she throws herself forward, crashing into my chest. I catch her when she bounces backward to stop her from falling.

"I'll do anything!"

I'm still holding her by the arms and she's trembling.

"Please, please, just let him go. It was just a stupid—"

"Since when is stupidity an excuse?"

"Please. I'll do anything you want."

I let silence hang in the air between us, watching her. "Anything?"

She pulls back and turns her face up and suddenly, I want to see her eyes. But then, she nods. Three quick, nervous little nods.

I touch her face, smear a tear down over her chin, her throat, to the hollow between her collarbones, the skin of her chest. She's holding her breath as I drag my finger down to where her blouse has torn a little, feel the softness of her breast. "Are you offering to fuck me, Priscilla?"

She draws back sharply. I watch her struggle to come to grips with what she's just done. I walk behind her and touch the ropes binding her wrists. "I'll have to see what's on offer, of course."

She makes a sound and I know she's crying again.

Slowly, I untie the rope and the first thing she does is reach up to her blindfold. I grip both wrists from behind.

"Don't do that," I whisper in her ear. "Not if you want to walk out of here."

Her hands shake but she nods and slowly sets her arms at her sides.

I move to stand before her.

"Show me."

"Wh...what?"

"Show me what it is you're offering."

Her mouth falls open like she can't believe what I just asked her to do. I don't actually expect her to do it. To strip. I can tell she's not that kind of girl. But when her trembling hands reach to draw her coat off her shoulders, I'm surprised. Hugo's watching her too but her brother's head's bowed. I can't believe he'd let his sister go through with this. Fucking asshole. When I'm done here, I think I'll break his arms too.

Priscilla's coat drops to the floor and she reaches for the buttons of her blouse. Tears are sliding down her face, but I can't stop watching as each button is slipped through its hole and she pulls open her blouse, then drags it off, letting it drop to the floor on top of her coat. She's wearing a pretty little white bra and I can see her hard, pink nipples through the lace.

Her hands move back and it takes her a minute to get her skirt unzipped. Once she's done it, she pushes it down over slender legs. She's wearing skin-colored thigh high stockings and I can see the neat mound of dark hair through the white lace of her panties.

She sets her hands on either side of her. I guess she thinks she's done.

"Continue."

"I...will you..." she's starting to hyperventilate.

"Your brother's a piece of shit. You sure he's worth this?" I can't help but ask. She reaches up to her face and I grab her wrists again, hold them between us. "U-uh." I don't want to have to hurt her. It doesn't feel right. "Get dressed and go home. Let your brother deal with the consequences of his actions."

"I can do this. I—I just need a minute. I just—"

"Cilla." It's Jones. We both turn to him.

"I—" Cilla starts, but stops.

"Go home, Priscilla. You don't belong here," I say.

"Please, I just..."

"You just what?"

Nothing.

I look her over. Something about her makes me curious.

"One month," I hear myself say.

"W...What?"

"You're mine for one month."

"I—"

"I own you for thirty days," I make very clear.

"I don't understand."

"I think you do. You have one minute to decide."

"What do I have to do?"

"Anything I want."

She knows my meaning.

I catch Hugo's eye because suddenly, there's nothing I want more than this. Her. One month. Her to myself. Mine.

When I give Hugo a nod, he cocks the gun. She jumps.

"Yes! Yes. Okay. One month. What you said. Please don't hurt him. Please."

Jones is quiet. I look away from her to him, grip a handful of his hair. "You going to let your sister do this?"

"I said yes!" his sister cries out. "Leave him alone!"

"Nothing?" I ask Jones.

He whimpers. Like the fucking coward he is. I take a deep breath in and lean in close so he and I are eye to eye. "I just need to know one thing before I take your sister to my bed."

His bloodshot eyes finally glide over to where she's standing beside us.

"Here, Jones. Focus here." I tug on his greasy hair until he looks at me. "Who put you in touch with the buyer?"

Nothing. Nothing but fear.

"Let me help you out. Was it my fucking cousin?"

He doesn't have to answer. I see the truth in his eyes. I release him and he falls backward.

"Please don't hurt him!" the girl cries out again. I turn to her. Pull her toward me so her chest is touching mine, so my cock is pressing against her belly. So she can get a feel for what she can expect. Her hands come up between us, a barrier. One I easily push aside.

"Pretty Priscilla," I start, reaching to undo the blindfold, dragging it slowly from her eyes. "So concerned for your brother. But aren't you afraid I'll hurt *you*?"

3

CILLA

I blink in the sudden bright fluorescent light. His fingers hover over what I know is a bump where the jerk in Jones's apartment slammed my head against the wall. It takes a moment for my eyes to adjust. I'm processing his words. His warning.

It's his chest I see first. Solid and thick. He's huge beneath the suit he's wearing. All black from head to toe. I pull my hands off, I'm afraid to look up. To see his face. His eyes. I'm terrified. He's a wall of muscle and power.

When I inhale, I smell aftershave, it's subtle but it's there. And as I stand here now, nearly naked, with him holding me like this, I know he *wi*ll hurt me.

But I have no choice.

I force my gaze upward. Neat stubble hones the already sharp line of his jaw. His hair is dark, almost black. I'm delaying having to meet his eyes, they're a blur in my periphery. His skin in smooth, but for the scar that spans his left cheek. No hair grows in that fine line and I know it was a knife that made it. That cut him like this. Another centimeter and he would have lost his eye.

I swallow, blink, force myself to look up, meet his eyes. Black or blue, I can't tell. Like a bruise. Like midnight. With an unmistakable edge inside them. A hardness. But something else too.

"Well?"

He's waiting for my answer. He won't take what I don't give but if I say yes, I will have to give. I'll have to give everything.

But what's the alternative? Standing by while he breaks my brother's legs? I can't do that. I won't. And this man knows that. "I agree to what you want."

He nods, but doesn't move. His eyes burn into mine and I have to blink several times. I can't hold his gaze. There's a hunger inside them. A fiery, almost demonic hunger. Like he's starved. Ravenous.

And I've just agreed. I've said yes.

I don't even know his name.

"Please let my brother go."

Without breaking eye contact, he gives a nod of his head and the other man shoves Jones forward. Jones stumbles, but doesn't fall. The gun is still at his back as the man follows him out.

"Is he worth it?" the beast before me asks, and suddenly, I feel like her. Like Belle, trapped, her life exchanged to save her father's. "Is he?"

Jones doesn't even look back.

"I don't know your name," I say.

"Kill."

I don't think he's even blinked. He's devouring me with his eyes. What will be left of me when he uses his hands? His mouth? His...

"Kill?" My voice breaks on the single syllable. What kind of name is that? Who names their son Kill?

I shudder.

He steps back, checks his watch.

"Hugo." The man who'd just escorted my brother out returns. Jones isn't with him.

"Sir," Hugo says.

"Take her to the penthouse. Put her in one of the bedrooms and post a man. Get her something for her head."

My head aches. He must know because he felt the bump there.

"Now?" He wants to take me now?

He barely turns back to me as he exits the room. "Not one of the idiots if you can manage it," he tells Hugo.

"But," I start, taking a step after him. Hugo steps between us. His eyes scan my nearly naked body and I cover myself with my arms.

He walks around me, picks up my discarded coat, puts it over my shoulders. "You don't want to catch a cold." His voice is grainier than Kill's. He pokes a finger into my back, my signal to move toward the door.

I turn to him. "Now? It starts now?" My insides are churning. I think I may puke, except I haven't eaten since breakfast. "I can't—"

"You agreed," he says, urging me forward. "One month. I wonder if you'll be walking when your time's up." He chuckles.

I glance over my shoulder but he's not looking at me. More men crowd the hallway and their gazes slide over me. These are dangerous men. The one hadn't hesitated to slam my head into the wall. And their leader—Kill—what won't he hesitate to do?

What did I agree to? What have I done?

I slip my hands into my coat and hug it to myself. I left the single shoe I was still wearing in the room so I'm barefoot but for the stockings which must have torn when they brought me here.

At the bottom of the stairs, Hugo puts a hand on my shoulder to stop me, and a moment later, he's sliding the wet blindfold back over my eyes.

"No." I touch the cloth, want to drag it off.

"It's either this or you ride in the trunk," he says, stepping into my line of vision.

I open my mouth to argue, but he raises an eyebrow and I know this is the end of the conversation. If you can call it a conversation. I drop my hands.

"Good girl."

I glare and he gives me a dark grin then secures the blindfold and guides me up the stairs. I grip the handrail, each of my steps heavier than the last. When I stumble, he catches me. A door opens and I hear music, people talking in low tones. Don't they see me here? Doesn't the sight of a woman being walked out like this, against her will, alarm them? Is this the norm for them? Blindfolded, bare-foot women guided out by these violent men? Where am I? What have I gotten myself into?

No, what has Jones gotten me into?

Had Kill said coke? Cocaine? Jones is clean. He swore it to me just last month. Did he lie?

A gust of cold, wet wind hits me. I hear a car's engine humming and brace myself to walk barefoot through icy puddles of water, but before I take one step, an arm wraps around my middle and I'm lifted up off the ground. I grip Hugo's forearm instinctively wanting to free myself, but he talks to another man there, giving instructions, then I'm placed on the leather seat. Hugo climbs in after me and closes the door. I take a breath and smell him, Kill. It's his aftershave. We must be in his car.

"Where's my brother?" I ask.

"You don't need to worry about him."

"How do I know he's safe?"

"When Kill makes a deal, he keeps it."

"How do I know that?"

"You don't."

I open my mouth to speak but a phone rings, and a moment later, he's talking and it's not to me. I turn my head toward the window, trying to see through the blindfold, but it's impossible. Instead, I try to make sense of what's happened since a few hours ago. I was supposed to be having dinner with my brother. That was all. Instead, I'm sitting blindfolded driving to what I assume is Kill's penthouse where God knows what will be expected of me.

No, I know what will be expected.

And the thought makes me shudder.

I guess it's half an hour before the driver slows and we pull into a garage. I know because the interminable rain has finally stopped pelting the windows. Hugo hasn't spoken to me and after that one call, he was silent.

Once we're parked, Hugo climbs out and his hand closes over my arm to drag me across the seat. I guess he's not worried about anyone seeing a blindfolded, bare-foot woman being escorted by a giant man because we're not rushing and he's even laughing at some lame joke the other man, I assume the driver, is telling. I hear a ding of an elevator and feel carpet beneath my feet when I step on. I'm glad for the carpet. I'm freezing even with my coat.

We ride up until the doors slide open. Once there, the blindfold comes off.

"Welcome home, at least for the next little while."

I gaze around the luxurious expanse of the space. It's huge. I wonder if it takes up the whole floor. And everything is shiny and sleek and looks like it's been freshly polished.

The elevator doors slide closed behind me and I turn, looking at the outline of my reflection, watching my freedom slip away. I stare at the blur of my face in the polished nickel.

"This way."

When I face him, I find Hugo watching me. I can't read him. I know he's as violent as the others but I also know he carried me to the car so I wouldn't have to step in puddles of water when we left wherever we were. He hasn't hurt me and I'm not afraid of him hurting me for some reason.

But he did hold a gun to my brother. He cocked it. Readied to pull the trigger.

He clears his throat.

I walk toward him, taking in my surroundings as I do. Is the elevator the only exit? No, there have to be stairs.

The long hallway holds six closed doors. He opens one, switches on the light and gestures for me to enter. It's a luxuriously decorated bedroom, everything in shades of cream, softer than I'd expect of the man I met. I take one step in but stop and turn to Hugo, panic taking hold of me. I shake my head and, without thinking, walk past him as if I have a choice. As if I will go back to the elevator and push the button and walk out of here. As if he'll let me.

He grabs my arm, his grip hard enough to warn me. "Don't make this hard."

I breathe fast, in and out, and my eyes heat up with tears. "Please don't make me."

"I'm not going to make you do anything but go into the bedroom." He studies me, lets me take in his words. "Have a bath. Relax. Kill will be here in a few hours."

How is he so calm?

Without waiting for me to reply, he turns me, places me inside the room.

"Aspirin should be in the bathroom. A man will be posted outside if you need anything. But try not to need anything."

"Wait!"

He's closing the door, but I wrap my hands around it so he's forced to stop.

He sighs, letting me know he's irritated.

"Can I call my brother? I can't just—"

"Don't make this hard."

His repeated words are a warning and I understand. I drop my hands and step back and watch the door close and lock and I don't hold back the tears when they slide down my face this time because I'm trapped. I'm finished. And I don't know if, once this month is up, I'll be walking out of here at all.

4

KILL

It's two in the morning when I get to the penthouse. I've been thinking about my pretty little captive all night. My dick's been hard with all the things I plan to do with her in the next month.

Although how tonight went down still baffles me. Why did I react the way I did to her? It's not like me. On the other hand, I'd rather fuck a beautiful woman than break some asshole's legs.

I dismiss the man standing beside the girl's door and pour myself a whiskey as I strip off my jacket and tie, and undo the top buttons of my black button down. I make my way down the hall to her room. Turn the key in the lock. Push the door open. The lights are still on but she must have been asleep because she startles awake. She's still got her coat on and I spy the torn stockings on her feet. She rights herself. She must have been sitting up waiting for me. But I'm not fool enough to think she did it because she couldn't wait for me to show up.

I stand back and sweep the arm that's holding the drink

toward the hallway. I'm wound up from the club. Need a little release before bed. There's never a shortage of women willing to suck me off, but I saved myself for her tonight. I wonder if she'd be grateful if I told her.

I decide not to.

Meanwhile, she's still sitting on the bed, arms folded across herself.

"You're stubborn, aren't you?"

She doesn't reply with words, just a glare.

"Where's my brother?"

"Safe."

"How do I know?"

"I give you my word."

"Like I said, how do I know?"

I feel my eyes narrow and bite back my response. She's already scared, no need to terrify her. It's right she'd have questions.

Only I don't like being questioned.

I take a step inside and drain my glass, watching her as I do. "I guess you'll have to trust me. What choice do you have?"

"I don't. You took that away."

"No, that's not accurate. *You* decided. *You* chose. And you can walk out of here anytime you like."

"At what price?"

"You can figure that out, can't you?"

"My brother."

"You're smarter than him. I can already tell. Now get up."

She drags her legs underneath her so she's kneeling up. "I have a job, you know."

"Good for you. I'm going to ask you nicely once more because you're new here. Get. The. Fuck. Up."

She considers, and I'm not sure if I'm disappointed that she does as I say and slides off the bed still holding her coat tight to her.

"Let's go have a drink." I stand aside, gesturing to the hallway again.

She moves, keeping her eyes on me as she passes and walks out into the hall.

I'm behind her, herding her to the living room. Once there, I pour her a whiskey and refresh mine. Handing it to her, I take a seat on the couch, leaning sideways, one arm splayed out over the back.

She stands awkwardly, holding her drink, unsure what to do.

"Drink it."

She takes a swallow, squeezes her eyes shut as it burns her throat. I smile.

"All of it."

She obviously isn't a whiskey drinker but she'll be more pliant with it in her. I wait while she drinks it down, making faces all along.

"Put the glass there." I point to the side table.

She obeys.

"Now let's see what's under that coat."

She starts trembling, her eyes going wide. They're a pretty shade of green, their brightness a stark contrast under the thick bangs of her almost black hair.

"What are you going to do to me?"

"Right now, I'm just going to watch you strip. Don't make me do it for you. You won't like that. Understand?"

She nods, or it's a tremble I mistake for a nod, but her hands move and she begins to unbutton her coat. It takes her a long time, she's shaking so hard, but eventually, she manages, and slides it off, then holds it in front of her like she doesn't know what to do with it.

"Put it down there." I point to a chair. I could give a fuck where she puts it but she needs specific instructions right now.

Once she's set the coat down, she stands waiting.

"Go on. Everything off." I sip my whiskey. Give her time to process.

She reaches back to unhook her bra and slowly slips the straps from her shoulders. She covers her tits as long as possible, but eventually, she has to let it drop. I wait, patient because watching her fight her inevitable submission is as arousing as seeing her naked. As imagining how her mouth is going to feel wrapped around my dick.

It takes her a full five minutes before she's standing with her arms at her sides, her eyes on a point somewhere beyond my shoulder.

"You need a lot of prompting. Most women are more...enthusiastic."

"Why don't you go find one of those women then?"

"Good one." I sip, studying her, then shrug a shoulder. "They're a dime a dozen. But you, Cilla—Jones told me you go by Cilla, is that right?" I don't wait for her to answer. "You will make the next month interesting." I drink another swallow. "Now show me your pussy."

She flushes red and it takes all I have not to laugh out loud. She strips off each stocking then slips her hands into the waistband of her panties and pushes them off, the swift movement angry. She balls it up and throws it at me.

"Happy?" she asks, folding her arms across her chest.

I catch her panties, bring them to my nose and inhale deeply. I let out a satisfied moan.

Her eyes go wide as she watches me. I guess she wasn't expecting that. I'm a dirty fuck though. She'll learn that soon enough.

I fold up the panties, tuck them into my pocket. I slide my gaze slowly to her pretty little pussy and examine it while she shifts on her feet.

"Hardly," I say in response to her earlier question. I painstakingly drag my gaze back up to hers, rise, walk to stand an inch from her. Her hands splay out on my chest to stop me from coming closer. Our eyes locked, I close my fingers over her pussy making her gasp. I'm surprised at the moisture, at the scent of arousal coming off her.

But I don't care about that just now. Now, I want her to heel.

I curl my fingers in the hair and tug. She winces, pushes at me.

"Do I need to teach you how to be respectful?"

She swallows. I squeeze.

"Do I?"

She shakes her head.

"Words."

"No."

I hold on a moment longer, then release her and step back.

"Good."

When I walk to the side table to refresh my drink, she remains standing awkwardly where she is. I resume my seat and sip. She wipes at her reddened eyes.

"Now turn around."

She does, and maybe she's glad to hide her face, so it's a win-win. I get a view of her gorgeous ass and she can hide from me when I give the next instruction.

"Spread your legs and bend over."

Her hands fly to her face and I can just imagine the expression on it. I sip my drink and give her a minute before reminding her of our deal.

"Anything. Remember that? You said you'd do anything. Are you changing your mind?" I grin, imagining her mortification. "Bend over and show me everything."

She continues to stand there, drops her arms to her sides. I think she's going to do it, she's building herself up, maybe giving herself a pep talk. What the fuck do I know? What the fuck do I care?

"Cilla."

Her hands fist at her sides, knuckles going white, and slowly, she turns to face me, her green eyes narrowed to cutting slits.

"You're a bully. You're no better than some rapist in a dark alley."

Everything changes in that moment. As soon as she utters that word, my vision goes red. I hear the pop of glass shattering, feel the sharp pain of shards slicing my hand, the liquor mixing with blood. She screams as I rise but strangely, my heartbeat hasn't changed. It hasn't accelerated. I'm calm. Controlled.

But at the same time, so completely out of control.

I take a step toward her and she takes off down the hall. I follow, stalking slowly, deliberately. She throws one look over her shoulder and slips into her room. I'm close though, so that when she slams the door, it bounces off the toe of my shoe.

She screams, backing away, stumbling, falling backwards on the floor.

"I'm not your whore!"

She scrambles up, frantically looking for something,

anything she can defend herself with. But she's no match for me. I'm about to drive that point home.

"You're exactly my whore," I say, each word deliberate. I wrap a hand around her throat, and, pressing her backward onto the bed, climb up to straddle her, trapping her thighs between my knees. I lean my face close to hers. I know what she sees in my eyes terrifies her. I see it.

"I'm not a rapist. You agreed. You knew *exactly* what you were getting into. What you put on offer."

She's clawing at my forearm, opening and closing her mouth. I squeeze, and she brings one hand to my face, her nails scratch my cheek, drawing blood.

Blood.

I blink.

I see it on her neck too from where my hand is bleeding from the broken glass. It's on her face. Her chest. Wherever my hands have been.

Her arm falls away and I look at her eyes. I release her throat, slide off the bed. She rolls onto her side coughing, gasping for breath. I take a step back, watching her, looking at the blood on her, on myself.

Giving a confused grunt, I turn, walk to the door. I stop there, my back to her. I run my hands over my face, through my hair. I force my legs to move, to get out of her room. Because I don't know what I'll do to her if I don't get the fuck out of her room.

Without turning back, I take hold of the doorknob. "Don't come out, understand? Do not come out of this room."

I slam the door shut and go into the living room, then through it and out onto the balcony. I don't care that it's pouring rain. That wind whips me like a lash. I don't care. I stand in it, letting it wash away the blood. Letting it pelt my face. I stand in it and remember and I can't think about anything else. Not the terrified girl in the bedroom. Not the fact that I almost killed her. Nothing.

Because all I see is blood. So much fucking goddamned blood.

5

CILLA

I lock the bedroom door. I know it won't keep him out, but I do it anyway. Trembling, shivering, fucking freezing, I back away, covering myself. I look down at my chest, see his prints in red. I raise my hand and find skin and blood under my fingernails.

What happened? What the fuck just happened?

What the hell have I gotten myself into? He's going to kill me.

I look around the bedroom. A bed, two nightstands, one on either side of the bed, a vanity, a dresser. I go to it, begin to shove it toward the door, but the thing must weigh a thousand pounds because I can't budge it. I give up, take the chair before the vanity and slide it beneath the doorknob. I don't think it'll hold if he wants to come in here, but it's something. I open every single drawer to find a weapon, something, anything I can use to defend myself, but come up short. In the bathroom, same thing. Bottles of shampoo and conditioner, bath wash and lotions, a toothbrush in its package, toothpaste. But nothing I can use to hurt him. Maim him.

Back in the bedroom, I listen for him. I force myself to put my ear to the door and hear nothing. There are two windows but we must be at least twenty floors off the ground. I'm not exiting that way.

He said I could leave anytime I wanted. I can't though. I know what that means for Jones.

Jones. Fuck. I'm so fucking stupid. He said he'd been clean for months and I believed him. Jones, my big brother. The one who gave up so much because of me. Who lost so much.

I sit on the edge of the bed. I remember what he went through at the house. I know why he's the way he is. He was brave once. Courageous. But that was beaten out of him good and hard.

Tears fill my eyes, wet my face. My stomach is empty but it feels like it's filled with bricks. This is an impossible situation. I have to do what he says. I have to give him anything he wants. Everything he wants.

What happened just now though makes me pause. He could have taken it tonight. He's bigger than me. Stronger than me. He could have made me, but he didn't. What was it that triggered his violent reaction? Not the word bully. He knows he's that. He doesn't care that he is that. Things changed when I accused him of being a rapist.

I stand, shaking my head to clear the image of that glass shattering in his hand.

He won't take what I don't give. But the question is, how long will he allow me to not give it?

I walk to the bathroom, lock the door behind me and switch on the shower. The water is steaming when I step under the flow. I wince at the heat but force myself to stay and when my body adjusts to the temperature, I wash away the blood, the skin under my nails. I scrub my hair and body and only switch off the water when I can't stand it anymore. I wipe the steam from the mirror before wrapping the towel around myself. My reflection looks back at me, my tired, reddened eyes, the bruises darkening in the shape of his fingers at my throat. I squeeze the moisture from my hair, wind it into a bun, use a rubber band I find in one of the drawers to hold it in place. I then tear open the toothbrush packaging and brush my teeth like a normal person. Like it's a normal night. Like I'm not trapped like some animal waiting her turn for slaughter.

When I return to the bedroom, the chair is still where I put it. He's not here. He didn't break down the door. He won't, I think. I think he was as shocked at his reaction as I was.

I pull back the thick, heavy comforter. It feels nice, luxurious. I climb into the bed naked because I have nothing to wear, but I don't switch off the lights and somehow, I drift off to sleep.

I WAKE BECAUSE I'M HUNGRY. FAMISHED, IN FACT. THE CLOCK tells me it's been almost twenty-four hours since I've eaten.

I rub my face and sit up, the events of the evening returning in vivid multicolor. How did I manage to sleep? I climb out of the bed, picking up the towel I'd discarded the night before and wrapping it around myself. It's still raining. Still gray. It's been raining for days. New York in the fall can be beautiful but when it rains like this, it kills me. I followed Jones here and not a day goes by where I don't wish he'd never moved away from Colorado.

But I can't leave him on his own. My being here, in this penthouse, under these circumstances, is evidence of that.

He's too vulnerable. Too breakable. I need to be there to put him back together if he breaks and I feel like he's always one step from shattering.

I go to the bathroom and brush my teeth, then walk to the bedroom door. After listening, making sure I hear nothing, I pull the chair out.

He told me not to leave my room but I have to. I don't want to. God, the last thing I need is to run into him. Break one of his rules. Will he still be angry? As angry? Will he have calmed?

I turn the doorknob, wincing at the pop of the lock releasing. It doesn't creak as I open it wide enough to peer into the hallway. It's empty. And it sounds like the entire penthouse is empty. There isn't even a guard stationed at the elevator.

The kitchen is at the other end of the living room. I'm just going to tip-toe in there, grab something to eat. I don't want to admit that I'm going to scurry back to my room like a frightened little mouse because that's exactly what I am right now. A scared shitless little mouse.

The apartment is dark. No lights are on and too many clouds hide the sun. I get to the kitchen and have to wonder if he ever eats in here. It's spotless. Not a crumb on any surface. I open the fridge, worried for a minute there won't be any food, but it's stocked. Shockingly full, actually. I'm about to take out a carton of juice when I hear the ding of the elevator and my heart lurches into my throat. I'm standing there, the carton in my hand in front of the refrigerator as the elevator doors slide open. A woman steps out and if she's surprised to find a stranger wrapped in a towel standing in the kitchen, she doesn't let on. It takes her all of one second to smile.

"Mr. Killian said he had company," she says.

She's older, maybe late fifties. And behind her a man in a suit steps off the elevator. Him I recognize. He gives me a nod. It's the man who smashed my head into the wall last night.

"It's raining cats and dogs out there," she says, setting her bag down on the kitchen counter while she takes off her coat. "Are you hungry?"

I'm so confused.

She comes around, takes the juice out of my hand, guides me to sit at the counter. She closes the refrigerator door.

"I'm Helen, honey. I cook and clean here. What's your name?"

"Um. I'm Priscilla." I shake my head. "Cilla." I haven't used Priscilla since...well, since mom died.

"Nice to meet you, Cilla. Now, Mr. Killian said I was to take care of you."

He did?

"What would you like to eat?"

"Uh...I can grab a...granola bar or something."

"Nonsense. How about an omelet?" She looks me over and I'm very conscious I'm wearing only a towel. "You're not one of those vegetarians, are you?"

Her expression puts me at ease, at least a little. "No. I'm not."

"Good. Why don't you get dressed and I'll make you a nice breakfast."

"Oh." I look around the living room for my coat, panties and bra. Find none of them. "I don't have any..."

"Just a minute."

Well, whatever she thinks of that information, she doesn't let on. Instead, she disappears down the hallway and returns a few minutes later with a bathrobe.

"You'll at least be more comfortable in this."

"Thank you."

She turns her attention to gathering the ingredients for my breakfast and I quickly slip the bathrobe on. I fold the towel and set it on the stool beside the one I sit on. The scent of bacon frying has my mouth watering.

"Is there a phone somewhere?" I ask, emboldened.

"Afraid not," she says, her back to me.

She doesn't embellish. I get the feeling she's been told not to let me use a phone if there is one.

"I just wanted to check on my brother," I try again. Maybe she has a cell phone she'll lend me.

"Well," she plates up an omelet so perfect, my stomach growls in anticipation. "Mr. Killian will be here soon. I'm sure you can ask him about that. Coffee?"

I nod and pick up my fork. *Mr. Killian will be here soon.* As hungry as I am, I have to force the food past the sudden lump in my throat.

Helen makes a cup of coffee and sets it in front of me. "Cream or sugar?"

"No, thank you."

"Well, I'd best get started. If you need anything else, holler."

"Thank you."

Helen disappears and I eat the plate of food, wondering about what's happening. If he told her to take care of me, then maybe he's calmed down? I'm thinking about that when the elevator dings again. I turn, sliding off my stool as Hugo enters followed by a man in a suit. He looks me over. Nods his greeting.

I stand there like an idiot.

"This is Doctor Horn. He'll be handling your exam," Hugo says to me.

"My exam?"

He turns to the doctor. He doesn't bother to introduce me.

"If I can set up?" the doctor asks Hugo.

"Third door on the right."

The room I'd slept in.

"What's going on?" I hug the lapels of the bathrobe to me as Hugo approaches. I take a step away when he veers left with a chuckle and goes to the coffee machine. He makes himself a cup and turns to me, leans against the counter, looks me over.

"What the hell happened last night?"

"What do you mean?"

"You did a number on Kill's face. Those scratches are usually on the back."

My mouth falls open but he just swallows his coffee and sets his cup in the sink.

"Let's go. We're on a tight schedule," he says, taking my arm.

"I'm not going anywhere with you. What exam? I have a doctor. I don't need—"

"You need to be checked for STDs and we need to make sure your birth control is up to date." He's dragging me toward the hallway.

"What? Oh my god. You're crazy!"

He stops.

"If you'd rather wait for Kill, we can do that. He'll be here soon. I'm sure after last night, he'll be very lenient."

I look at his face, his eyes. They're hard. He's not messing around. I move when he begins to walk.

"I don't need an exam," I try, but I know my words fall on deaf ears.

In my bedroom, Dr. Horn has stripped the bed of everything but one pillow. He's also set up his tools on a tray beside the bed. I recognize all the implements. My gynecologist uses them when I go in for my annual visits.

"Please disrobe and lie on the bed."

Hugo has released my arm but I stiffen at the order. When I back away, I hit his wall of a chest.

"Do as you're told and don't waste the doctor's time."

Dr. Horn looks at me. "It's just an examination. Routine."

"It's not routine. I don't need—"

Hugo picks me up by the arms and carries me to the bed. I'm fighting but it's useless. Once there, he sits me on the edge and takes my chin in his hand, forcing me to look at him. "I can tie you spread eagle to the bed or you can lay back and do what the doctor says and have it over with. This is happening. You decide how it's happening."

Instinct takes over and I try to make a run for it. Logic isn't working because if it were, I'd know I have no chance of escape. I kick and scream as Hugo hauls me onto the bed and links my hands with a set of leather cuffs already attached to the top of the bed. Once I'm secured, he grabs one kicking leg at the ankle and drags it wide, his cold eyes on mine as he does. He links it to the cuff there. I'm still fighting when he takes the other leg and does the same. I'm spread wide, the robe barely covering the essentials, but Hugo keeps his eyes glued to mine as he unties and opens it wide, exposing me to him, to the doctor, to anyone who chooses to walk by the open door.

He then shakes his head at me. "She's all yours, Doc." He moves to the far wall where he'll have an unobstructed view between my legs, and folds his arms across his chest as he leans against it and watches. I see Helen walk by the door but she doesn't glance inside. She's whistling and carrying on with her cleaning as if this is totally normal.

Dr. Horn's gloved fingers press against me, opening my folds, smearing lubricant into me. I squeeze my eyes shut, hate the tears that slide from their corners as he does his work, taking a smear. It's over within moments. I open my eyes to watch him place the sample in his bag and retrieve two syringes.

"What are those for?"

"Birth control and a blood sample."

He comes to the top of the bed and I start to struggle. Hugo steps forward.

"Blood first," the doctor says.

Hugo grips my arm so hard, I can't move it. It hurts when the doctor sticks the syringe in, taking the sample. When Hugo releases me, I do the only thing I can. I open my mouth and bite his hand.

"Fuck." He swipes it away.

It wasn't even hard enough to draw blood.

"I can shoot this one into her hip if you turn her over and hold her still."

"With pleasure." Hugo uncuffs one leg, but his grip is so tight as he folds it over the other, that I can't move it at all. I feel the cold cotton swab readying the area and flinch when the needle penetrates skin. I'm so caught up in what's happening to me that I don't even hear Kill when he enters the room.

"She's compliant, I see," he says when the doctor pulls the needle out and Hugo releases me so I roll onto my back.

"That's her. Compliant," Hugo deadpans.

I look at the scratches down Kill's face. I got him good. But I know he'll get me better.

I meet his eyes. The rage of last night is gone. He still looks terrifying even wearing the expensive suit, but he's not out of control. He shakes the doctor's hand.

"Thank you, Dr. Horn. Your services are appreciated as is your discretion."

"Of course, Mr. Black."

Mr. Black?

But I don't have time to think about this now because Kill turns his full attention to me, looks me over, walks to the bed, and sits on the edge of it. His gaze wanders over my naked body, pausing at my sex before his eyes meet mine.

"I'm going to teach you to obey me," he says, and I know he hasn't forgotten what happened last night. He undoes my still bound leg, then my wrists. I sit up, rub them, cover myself as best I can. From inside his jacket pocket, he takes out a cell phone, scrolls to a number and dials it, then hands me the phone.

I take it, confused, put it to my ear.

"Cill?" It's Jones.

"Oh, God. Jones." Relief washes over me and tears warm my eyes. "Are you okay?"

"Yeah. I'm okay, sis. Are you?"

I glance at Kill. I'm not sure how to answer that. "Where are you?" I ask instead.

"I can't say, but I'm safe. I guess he needs you to know that."

"Are they hurting you?"

"No."

I nod, but he can't see me.

"Sis, you shouldn't have done that," he says.

I'm crying, wiping my face with one hand, pressing the phone to my ear with the other.

"There. You know he's not hurt. Now say goodbye," Kill says.

My eyes snap to his.

"One month. You'll see him after that," he says.

I study him, trying to gauge if he's telling the truth, that he's not going to hurt Jones. Jones sounds okay though. Not under duress.

"I have to go," I say. "I'll see you again when this is over, okay?"

"I'm sorry," Jones says. "I'm sorry for being an idiot."

"You're not an idiot."

"Say goodbye," Kill repeats.

"Goodbye."

Kill takes the phone and puts it into his pocket. He gets off the bed. "Get dressed. We're leaving." He motions to the shopping bag I hadn't noticed.

"Leaving?"

"We're taking a trip."

"Where to? I have a job. Rent." I'm a freelance journalist, but still. I need to work to pay the bills.

"You told me that last night. I took care of everything. All you have to worry about for the next month is pleasing me. You do that, and all will be well."

"You said I could leave." I don't know why I bring that up. I won't leave. I know that.

"I changed my mind." He gives me a long look, then turns and walks out the door, closing it behind him.

6

KILL

Not fifteen minutes later, Cilla walks out of her bedroom and into the living room. She's dressed in jeans, a sweater and a pair of knee-high boots I ordered for her from a nearby boutique. I got the size right. The jeans hug her tight ass and the cashmere sweater displays the small, soft curves of her breasts. The deep crimson sets of her olive skin and dark hair. She's not wearing makeup and still she's stunning.

I nod in approval and finish my cup of coffee. Helen takes it from me and I retrieve the black wool coat and hand it to Cilla.

"I have clothes," she says, looking at the coat but not taking it.

"When you receive a gift, you say thank you."

"I never asked for a gift."

"That's the definition of a gift, isn't it? A thing given willingly without the expectation of payment."

"But there will be payment."

I give her a one-sided grin. "Coat. It's cold out." I'm now holding it for her to slide her arms into it.

"Where are we going?" she asks, taking the coat from me and putting it on herself.

"Sleepy Hollow." I don't look at her when I say it. I don't even know why I'm taking her there. I haven't been back in years. Part of me wants to go. To see it again. But another part, maybe the smarter part, says stay the fuck away from the past.

"Sleepy Hollow?" She's scrunching up her face, confused.

I nod and gesture to the man standing at the elevator that we're ready to go. The doors slide open a moment later and I nod in the direction of the elevator.

She moves into it. "How long will we be there? What's up there anyway?"

"You ask a lot of questions." We're riding down to the garage.

"Give me one answer and I'll stop."

I turn to her, my gaze sweeping over her face. "My house."

"I thought this was your house."

"My other house."

Her eyebrows shoot up. She's quiet until the doors slide open and we're at the garage.

"I'll drive myself," I tell the driver waiting beside the SUV. My head's in a weird place. It's like I'm talking and moving, but it's not me. Like I'm watching myself go through the motions because I'm trying to make sense of what the hell I'm doing. Why I'm going back. "Is everything in order at the house?"

"Yes, sir. Ready for your arrival."

I look at Cilla, take her arm to walk her around to the passenger side, open the door and gesture for her to get in.

"Why are we leaving the city? What did you mean you took care of everything?"

"Because I want to and I mean your rent is paid and apartment secured while you're away. As far as work, you're a freelance journalist. You can write when I don't require your…services."

That last part makes her stop. "Am I going to be safe?" she asks finally, quietly.

"Finally a question that matters." I give her a cold grin. "You will be safe, but you will also be obedient. You made the trade to save your useless brother's legs. You offered up anything I want. This is what I want. Now get in."

She climbs into the truck. I close the door and walk to the driver's side, taking my time. I take the keys from the man I'd usually have driving me, get in and start the engine.

"Can I at least stop by my apartment and get some clothes? My laptop?" she asks. "I mean, if we'll be there for a while."

She's fishing for information, but thing is, I don't have it. Not even for myself.

"I'll get you what you need."

She sighs, looks ahead as we pull out of the garage. It's so quiet for the first fifteen minutes that I switch on the radio to break the silence.

"He's not useless," she says when I do.

"What?"

She's not looking at me. "Jones. He's not useless. You don't know anything about us."

"I know he was willing to let his sister sell herself to save his ass. I'm being kind when I use the word useless."

She turns to me, her gaze fiery. "Like I said, you don't know anything about us."

"Then enlighten me. It's a long drive."

She shakes her head. "Why did you have a doctor check me out?"

I glance at her. She's looking straight ahead. "You don't think all I'll expect from you is conversation, do you?"

"No, I don't. I'm not stupid, you just could have asked."

"I'd rather be certain."

"What about me?" she asks, defiance in her tone. She's shifted in her seat to look at me now. "What if I want you tested?"

I give her a wide, toothy grin. "I'm clean."

"I'd rather be certain."

"You're going to be fun."

Her shoulders slump as she leans back in her seat and watches traffic crawl by.

I turn my attention to the road too, my mind busy. Hugo arranged for a cleaning crew to get the house ready for us early this morning. It'll take more than a few hours to clean all the rooms though. So much has been shut up. Helen, who worked for my father and then my uncle, will travel to the house later today as well. I know she's gone back to the place since that night. Someone had to make sure of the upkeep. When I told her I wanted to return to Rockcliffe House early today, she just looked at me for a few minutes before nodding her head, telling me she'd be ready to go this afternoon.

I glance over at my passenger. She's wrong about me not knowing anything about her or her brother. I know they grew up in foster homes, their parents having been killed when Jones was fourteen and she was twelve. No relatives to take them in and too old for adoption. They bounced around for the first two years, but then stayed with one family until Jones's eighteenth birthday where he was granted guardianship of his sister. Ironically, the judge who did that was also the man with whom they both had lived for the last two years of their time in the system. And what did Jones do after that? He fucked up over and over again, and his little sister cleaned up for him over and over again.

Given all of that, this should feel like a fucking vacation to her, and me, I'm her fairy fucking godmother.

Traffic slows us down but when I finally pull off the exit and see the familiar sign to Sleepy Hollow, I feel my gut churn. I want to turn around. Go back. Forget about coming here, but I keep driving. My hands tighten around the steering wheel as we pass gated mansions spread farther and farther out as I approach Rockcliffe House. Cilla is sitting up, really paying attention now. I wonder if she's memorizing the road. Maybe thinking she'll have a chance to run. She won't. I'll make that clear when we reach Rockcliffe House.

The tall iron gates finally come into view. They're supported on either side by a large, stone pillar which becomes a six-foot high perimeter surrounding the property. Each of the pillars is topped with a watching gargoyle. And they are truly watching. Cameras are embedded within each one.

I slow the SUV and turn onto the path leading to those foreboding gates.

"*This* is your *house*?" she asks, her eyes on the gates, on the turret just visible over the hill behind them.

I don't answer, only because I can't. It's taking all I have to keep breathing. Keep calm.

When we reach the closed gates I stop, punch in a code. The tall iron creaks as they slowly open.

I navigate the SUV through and movement in the rear-view mirror tells me the gates are already closing behind us. Cilla's leaning forward in her seat to watch now, her mouth slightly open. I keep my eyes on the road even as the house comes into view, casting its shadow over us, bringing memories long forgotten into the foreground of my mind. I pull to a stop before the entrance and switch off the engine. I look around at the overgrown lawn, wet with all the rain we've had. I remember playing in it as a kid. Remember Ginny and me out here for hours and hours. We only had each other. Given my family's line of work, we grew up on our own. Home-schooled, and essentially friendless. Becoming more and more isolated as the years went by and my father's paranoia deepened. Although, I guess it wasn't paranoia. Not after what happened to mom.

I clear my throat and steel myself before turning to Cilla.

"Welcome to Rockcliffe House." Her mouth is still open. I reach over, put a finger under her chin and close it.

She draws back. "This isn't a house. I guess I have no idea how much money thugs make these days."

I could take offense, but honestly, I need her distraction right now, so I chuckle.

"You're pushing your luck, sweetheart." I get out of the car and walk around to her side. She's already got the door open and is climbing out.

"Are you going to lock me away from the world for the next thirty days?"

I wrap a hand around the back of her neck and guide her toward the large wooden doors. "It's tempting to have you at my beck and call." I stop walking and turn to her, make her face me. My grip is just tight enough to warn. "But you already are. Don't forget why you're here. Don't make the mistake of thinking you're anything other than mine. Mine to do with as I please. What happened last night will not happen again. Am I clear?"

She's watching my face, studying my eyes. Trying to read

me. "Or what?" she asks, but her voice is higher than usual, giving away her anxiety.

I lean in close so our noses touch. "Test me and you'll find out. Please."

We stay like that for a long minute, and I'm pretty sure she only breathes when I release her. We turn to the front doors that are pushed open, two men standing at attention just inside.

"Boys." I nod in greeting, my tone casual although the old, closed up smell of the house still carries something familiar in it. My cell phone vibrates in my pocket. I fish it out. It's Hugo. I silence it, but need to call him back.

Cilla's looking around, her eyes like saucers. The formal living room and the dining room, both of which we can see standing in the foyer, have been thoroughly cleaned, and I remember how my mother had wanted to replace the carpet in the dining room where a spill stained it. She never got the chance though.

I turn my gaze to the curving staircase, wide and opulent, the steps white marble veined with black to match the foyer.

"Is the blue bedroom prepared?" I ask.

"Yes, sir."

"Please take my guest to it. Assign a man to her room in case she needs anything or feels the need to go wandering about."

She gives me a glare but her curiosity has her following the man up. I head to my father's study, blocking the memories from my mind. I don't have time to deal with them just yet. I'll work now. Give myself until tonight. Then I'll go out back. Out to the barn. The greenhouse my mom had such hopes for. Then I'll stand inside and let myself remember.

7

CILLA

I walk into the blue bedroom and don't turn around when the door closes behind me. I have too much on my mind and I know the man will stand guard outside. I know I won't be allowed out until Kill comes for me. But for right now, that's okay. I need to process what's happened. Who I'm dealing with. Because I've just realized who he is.

I go to one of the three windows lining the walls and push it open. My room overlooks the back of the property. I know the layout of the house. I've studied the design. Was obsessed with it for a time.

I leave the window open even though it's cold out because the room has a smell to it. The whole house does. It's like the stain of the past. Of secrets being locked away for too long. It's stale and decrepit even though the mansion is in excellent condition. I try to imagine what it must cost to maintain it. Wonder how often Kill comes here. It's a hell of a weekend getaway.

Keeping my coat on, I let fresh, cold air into the bedroom and look around. The Persian carpet is slightly worn but in good condition, and pretty. A light blue with elaborate, beautiful patterns along the four corners. I go to the bed, pull back the duvet, and sit. It's much more comfortable than I expect it to be, but the mattress is new, even though I can tell the bed is an antique. It has four posts and a canopy over the head. I smell the comforter, the pillow. They don't smell like the room. These are new.

I open the single drawer in the nightstand and a pencil rolls forward. It's kind of creepy, the sound. I pick it up. It's only about three inches long and the eraser has been chewed on. I wonder about the person who did that. If it was her. Kill's sister, Virginia. Ginny for short. I put it back and close it.

There are two doors and I open the first one to find a bathroom. It's large and luxurious, although the fixtures are old. Fresh towels are stacked on a shelf with bottles of shampoo, conditioner, soap, and anything I could ask for, really. I recognize the brands too. Nothing I can usually afford to buy.

Back in the bedroom, I open the other door and a light goes on. It's a large walk-in closet. And it's stocked. Hanging on a rack are too many dresses for me to count. Shoes are lined neatly on shelves along another wall and the drawers are filled with jeans, sweaters, shirts, belts, underthings. I check the labels. Look at the tags. Everything is new and everything is my size.

I step back, confused. There are more clothes here than in my closet at home.

Back in the bedroom, I pull my coat tight around me as a gust of cold wind blows in rain and a few yellowed leaves from the tree outside. I go to it, let my face get wet as I survey the property. It's vast, although needs maintaining. Everything is overgrown and melds into the thick cropping of trees at the far end. The pool is unprotected. The tarp is torn and weather-worn. Leaves lie inside, rotting in stagnant rain water. The abandoned feel of the place gives me a chill and I draw the window closed. I lean my back against the wall, hugging my arms to myself.

I wonder why he brought me here.

It's all coming together now. Who he is. What this place is.

About two years ago, I'd done a story on haunted mansions in the northeast for a Halloween ghost story. Rockcliffe had become the headliner of my piece with not one ghost but two.

Earlier, when the doctor had called Kill by his last name, it wasn't that I recognized it, but it had jogged something in my brain. Kill. Mr. Killian. Mr. Black. Kill is Killian Black. His family is notorious. His father and uncle were both criminals with ties to the mafia. Killian now runs Mea Culpa, a high end gentlemen's club, essentially a strip club for the elite, which I was sure was used as a front to launder money. That's where I must have been yesterday, where they'd taken Jones and me. That would explain the music. And why no one cared that I was being led out so obviously against my will.

The only photographs I had ever seen of Kill when I'd found the house and my interest had been piqued had been taken when he wasn't quite eighteen. The way he looked then versus the way he looks now, you wouldn't say it was the same person.

Although, the piece I wrote was essentially fiction but for a handful of facts, when I'd been researching Rockcliffe House, I learned about the Black family's tragic history. Killian's father and uncle had been enemies, but when his father had died, his uncle had been granted custody of him and Ginny. Kill would have been sixteen at the time and Ginny fifteen. The tragedy had come almost two years later when, in the same week, Kill's sister hanged herself in the barn which had been partially converted into a greenhouse on the property, and his uncle had been found brutally murdered. The shock had come when Killian had been arrested for his uncle's murder. He'd been two weeks' shy of his eighteenth birthday, and was tried as an adult, sentenced to a twenty-four year prison term.

But only four years later, he was free. Only four years for a brutal act of murder. Both the suicide and the murder had taken place on the property only days apart. I'd tried to gain access to the trial records, but the case had been sealed and this house had sat empty, I guessed apart from maintenance judging from the state it was in, since the day Killian had been taken into custody.

Kill's uncle's death, like so many things, got lost in the weeks following as other news stories took over the headlines. And no matter how much I dug, I couldn't find anything more about the story and I knew there was a cover-up.

And now I stand wondering why in hell he's brought me here.

DAY TURNS INTO NIGHT BEFORE I HEAR HIS VOICE IN THE hallway. I get up from my place on the bed and want to put my boots back on, but don't have a chance to before the door opens and Killian Black stands in it, looking like a giant, a formidable force. He's no longer wearing his suit jacket or tie and his shirt sleeves are rolled half-way up thick, tattooed forearms. The top two buttons are undone and I see the dark ink of another tattoo on his chest.

I've been thinking about how to handle this the whole day. Wondering if I should tell him I know who he is. Know what he did. But when I see him, it's like all my courage dissolves.

Kill walks inside and looks around the room. I wish I'd had time to put on the boots because I'm two inches shorter without them and I need the height with him. Seeming satisfied with the room, he looks me over.

"Your STD test came back negative."

"I could have told you it would."

He glances up at the canopy over the bed before returning his gaze to me. "Are you comfortable?"

"Is this where I'll be locked up for the next thirty days?" I don't know why I'm being combative. It's like I can't control the words as they come hurtling out.

He steps closer, a devilish grin playing on his lips, and takes my arms, rubbing them up and down—he's holding back, I can tell—before closing his hands over them. "There are less hospitable rooms."

"I'm sure there are."

"You're ungrateful."

"I know who you are."

He studies my face, searches my eyes. I don't know what I expect him to say, not sure he realizes I mean I know what he did. Not when he doesn't acknowledge my comment.

"Dinner's ready. We'll talk about rules and expectations after we eat. You're hungry, I presume." Someone had come up with food earlier but I'd turned it away out of pure stubbornness and regretted it later because they hadn't asked me twice.

I nod, because the growling of my stomach tells him yes, I'm starving.

He walks into the closet and returns a moment later with a dress. It's a calf-length pale violet dress with spaghetti straps. He tosses it on the bed along with a pair of strappy sandals.

"Change."

I look at it, then at him. "It's cold for that, don't—"

"Change."

I exhale, and pick up the dress, making a point of checking the size, turning my nose up at it even though it's beautiful. "Can I have some privacy?" I ask finally.

"No."

My jaw tightens.

"This can go like last night went, but if that happens, it'll be me stripping you and taking you downstairs to eat naked in front of the staff."

I swallow. His tone is just this side of controlled. My hands shake as I pull my sweater over my head, then push my jeans off. I take the dress off the hanger and go to slip it on but he stops me.

"Nothing underneath."

I look up at him, then down, closing my eyes for a moment before reaching back to undo my bra. He watches silently as I take it off. I then slide off my panties, everything feeling like déjà vu. It's humbling, this re-enactment of the night before. I pull the dress over my head. The silk is cool against my skin, and my nipples push against the fine material. It comes to just past my knees and is a perfect fit. I sit on the bed to slip on the sandals. He watches me quietly and when I stand, he looks me over, gives me a nod and gestures to the door.

"Let's go," he says.

I walk ahead of him out into the now abandoned hallway, acutely aware of his eyes on me, a fine layer of silk the only thing protecting me from his gaze. For now. We go down the stairs. As we near the lush dining room, the smell of dinner makes my stomach groan again. If he hears, he doesn't say anything.

The dining room table is a rectangle that can seat about sixteen. Two places are set, and when we reach them, Kill pulls out my chair. I sit and watch as he takes his place at the head of the table. The large crystal chandelier blinks once. We both glance up at it.

It's strange to look at him now. He seems so civilized, so different from the man I met just yesterday. The man who had my brother and I kidnapped, who threatened to break his legs. A man who deals in drugs and sex. Who makes trades that save one man's legs from being broken in exchange for the ownership of another's body.

"What are you thinking?"

I shake my head, realize I've been staring at him. "Nothing."

He takes the open bottle of red and pours us each a generous glass.

The kitchen door opens and Helen, the woman I'd met earlier in Kill's penthouse, enters, followed by two young girls in uniforms. One is carrying a large, closed serving dish from which wafts the most delicious smell of beef and spices. The second girl has a plate of roasted vegetables. Helen directs them to set the dishes down and removes the lid from the main dish.

"Mmm, my favorite, Helen." Kill closes his eyes as he savors the scent.

Helen smiles and I know she's been with him for a long time. She knows him. And he seems to trust her. "I figured homecoming required a special meal. Girls." The two girls begin to serve us. They fill Kill's plate first, then mine, and I can't help but appreciate the exotic scent wafting up from my dish.

Once they've served us, they leave us alone. Kill takes his napkin and places it on his lap. He glances at me over a forkful of food. "Eat."

I follow his lead and take my first bite and oh my goodness. It's heaven. The meat melts on my tongue, the flavors exploding, tasting like nothing I've eaten before.

"Helen is an amazing cook. She's been with my family for years."

"Are we going to make small talk?" I ask. "I mean, let's be straightforward about the fact that I'm here against my will. This isn't exactly a date."

"Oh, I wouldn't be anything but straightforward. But I like to take care of my things. Don't want them breaking down. Passing out. Fading away with hunger. What would be the point?"

I set my fork down. I've lost my appetite. His reminder is blunt, cutting.

He sips his wine and takes another bite. "Don't pout, Cilla. It's not becoming."

"What do you want with me? You can have anyone you want. You have a strip club full of women I'm sure would love to be here in my place right now. What do you want with me?"

He tilts his head to the side as he chews another forkful. I realize I've given something away. I shouldn't know about Mea Culpa. I'm sure that's where I was when I was blindfolded, but I shouldn't know it. And from the look on his face, he didn't miss my slip.

I clear my throat and force a potato into my mouth.

"We made a deal. I want what you promised. And in return, I'll keep my promise. That's all."

"There's a closet full of clothes upstairs."

"If you prefer to walk around the house naked, that's certainly—"

"I know who you are," I blurt out, wanting a reaction. "I know what you did."

He considers me, his eyes clouding, darkening. Like they did last night before he attacked me. I wring the napkin in my hands and push my chair back a little, readying to run. But where? Where would I run to?

Kill takes the last bite of food, cleaning his plate, then wipes his mouth and sets his napkin on the table. He rises and looks down at me.

I push my chair farther back and stand. He leads the way out of the dining room, past the living room and to another door. When he opens it, I stand in awe. It's a library. A fully stocked library with high oak shelves and arched, leaded windows. This room must not have a floor above it because the ceilings are high on one half and a staircase leads to a balcony on the other with more books lining the circular back wall.

Kill walks inside and moves directly to a cart of liquor. He pours two glasses of whiskey and turns to me. "Come inside and close the door."

I do. It's darkly intimate with only three lamps providing the softest light.

He points to the leather armchair and I sit, taking the drink he holds out to me. He remains standing.

"Rules for the time you spend at Rockcliffe House. You're allowed to come into the library whenever you like. You can spend as much time in here as you want. Same with your bedroom. When you're hungry, go to the kitchen and Helen will prepare something for you. When I require your presence for a meal, you'll dress as you are tonight."

"You mean almost naked."

"You'll curb your tongue when speaking with me. From this moment forward, I will punish you when you aren't respectful. Am I clear?"

"Punish me how?"

One side of his mouth curves upward. "I'll show you. I'm sure an opportunity will present itself soon."

I don't want him to see how his warning impacts me, but I know he sees my shudder.

"You'll be allowed outside twice a day with supervision."

I open my mouth to remark on that, but close it again. I'm not sure I want to learn about his punishments just yet.

"Questions so far?"

"Will I be here for the full month?"

"I haven't decided."

"You said I'd be able to work. I need my laptop to do that."

"Once you earn it, you'll have it."

"But you said—"

"Thirty days. Our agreement. It was your idea, remember. You're mine for the next thirty days." There's a pause while he drinks, his eyes watching me all along. "I don't want you wandering around the house alone. Bedroom, library and kitchen only. Clear?"

"Clear." I say what he wants to hear.

"Good. Finish your drink."

As if to set the example, he drains his glass. I know what's coming after this. And I know there's no way to get out of it. My heart is racing and goosebumps make the hair on my arms stand on end. I finish my drink and set it down on the side table beside me.

"Come here, Cilla."

I just look at him for the longest time. My insides are churning. I have a thousand questions and none that matter. Because what's left for me to ask?

I am his whore.

It's what I offered. What it cost to save my brother. Maybe after this, I'll be finished owing Jones, but I know that's not true. I'll never be finished. So I do as Kill says. I rise to my feet and go to him.

"Closer," he whispers.

I move one more inch. The toes of my sandals are touching his shoes, my nipples brushing his chest. I have to crane my neck to look up at him.

"I won't ever want you, you know," I start. "I won't ever give it. Know that you'll have to take it every time."

He cocks his head to the side, his gaze unreadable, intense. "Maybe I like taking, Cilla."

"I hate you."

"That's a shame."

"I'll never enjoy it. You'll always know that you forced me. That you hurt me."

"Kiss me."

A kiss? Just a kiss? I expected him to push me to my knees. To use my mouth in other ways. But a kiss, it's intimate. More intimate than other things. And the command makes me shudder.

"Kiss me," he repeats.

He wants a kiss. It's not a fuck, is it? It's not that. Why does this feel like so much more than that? Why does it make me feel so much more vulnerable?

When I don't move, he wraps a hand in my hair, tilts my head back and kisses me. We're close. So close, I can see specks of gold in his dark eyes. I want to close mine, feeling too naked. Too exposed. But I don't. I won't. I have to watch him, like he's watching me.

The softness of his lips surprises me. It's such a contrast to the stubble that's scratching my cheek, my chin. To the fingers tugging my head back. Such a contrast to everything this man is.

I take his lower lip between mine, tasting whiskey as I kiss him. Taste him.

Sink my teeth into him.

He groans. His hardness presses against my belly. It's thick and big. I meant to hurt him. To make him flinch. But I seem to have done the opposite. When his hand closes over my hip, I draw back, breaking the kiss, my breathing coming hard, my heart beating fast.

Kill looks down at me, his pupils dilated, eyes glistening. He moves his hand from my hip to capture my wrist and turns my palm to him, wrapping it over his erection.

I gasp and try to pull free and the spell is broken.

"Let me go." My voice comes out strange, not high, but low and quiet.

"Make me."

I look at the scratches down his face. Look at the deeper one, the permanent one. Did someone else try to make him before?

"Make me let you go, Cilla."

I squeeze my hand around his cock, but it only makes him moan with pleasure, makes him swell in my palm. And when I try to pull away again, he twists my wrist, drawing me even nearer, our bodies pressing against each other.

"Fight. You want to," he says, his voice also low and deep, barely a whisper.

"It's what you want. I told you I'll never give you what you want."

Even as I say it, I know I'm a hypocrite because I am fighting, trying to free myself, I know it's useless. I know the only way I'll be free is when he frees me. And some part of me, it wants this. Some sick, destructive part of me wants exactly this.

Kill slides his free hand along my thigh, bunches up the silk as he hikes it up, all the while our eyes locked. But when he cups my sex, I go completely still.

"Why did you do it?" he asks.

"What?" I can't breathe. Not when he's holding me like this.

"Why did you come here? Why did you agree?"

Why did I offer myself in exchange for my brother? That's what he's asking?

I slide my gaze away. I can't answer that. I won't.

I shake my head once, he moves his fingers. I bite my lip.

"You're wet, Cilla."

"No."

He grins. "Again," he says. "Kiss me again."

I begin my struggle anew, knowing I have to get away. To free myself. Because this man, he does something to me. Something wicked. A thing that will break me because he was right last night. I am a whore. I'm exactly *his whore*.

"No. Never."

I break free and, before I can think, I raise my arm to slap him. I know he can stop me. I know because I hesitate, but he doesn't. He doesn't stop me and the sound my hand makes when it collides with his face is deafening. He flinches, but barely. When I prepare to do it again, though, he catches my wrist.

"Let me go!"

He's watching me with that grin, the one that says 'I know I'll win'. The one that says, 'I already have'.

Any momentary tenderness is replaced by dominance. By ownership. I lock eyes with him again, but this time, it's like predator and prey. And I am firmly cornered. Caught.

"You want this, Cilla. You want this exactly like this."

"I don't."

He walks me backward until my back hits the wall. That's when he releases my sex, grabbing my hips instead, raising me up, fingers digging into me. I know he's right. That I'm wet. He keeps me there with one hand while with the other, he undoes his belt, his pants, pushes them down. I look at his cock. It's thick and big. Too fucking big, the bulbous head glistening with pre-cum.

"Wait," I gasp, but he grips my legs, widening them, setting them around his hips. I feel him at my entrance and I'm sucking in air as I cling to his shoulders, his neck. "I—"

"Shh. It's okay to want, Cilla."

He's taunting me and I hate him for it. For his control over me.

He closes his mouth on mine, biting my lip. I taste the metallic taste of blood.

He's wrong. I don't want this. I swear I don't. I *can't* want it.

My eyes are closed, and when I open them, I find him watching me.

"Cilla," he says, his voice a hoarse whisper as he drives into me, his full length plunging too deep too fast. I'm not ready, even aroused—because I am aroused—I'm not ready, and I cry out.

He moans at the sound and slides out, then thrusts again. One hand is wrapped around my hip, with the other, he tears the dress apart and takes my breast between his fingers, kneading it, then gripping the nipple between thumb and forefinger, drawing it out as he thrusts again.

I gasp but the pain and pleasure, they're confused. My clit is rubbing against him, his cock is splitting me in two and with his fingers punishing my nipple, I'm going to come. I don't want to, don't want to give him the satisfaction, but I'm slick and he's fucking me harder, faster, and his eyes are watching me. Seeing me.

Fuck.

He closes his mouth over mine again and when he groans and stills and I again taste blood, I suck in a desperate breath and I come. I come as he empties inside me, filling me as he throbs against my contracting walls, his eyes shining, bright, his voice low and deep when he says my name, and I finally close my eyes, unable to hold his, hating myself for coming, for giving over to this pleasure, a pleasure that belongs to him.

Like me.

Like I belong to him.

He pulls out and a gush of liquid slides down my thighs. I look at the mixture of blood and cum. I'm not a virgin, but he was too big, too violent. My knees buckle when my feet hit the floor but he catches me. I slump into him, the top of my head in his chest. I am ashamed. I am...vanquished.

Kill wraps a hand around my throat and forces me to look at him, holding me up against the wall. His grip isn't choking, but it can be. At any moment, he can snap my neck.

He looks at my mouth and I touch my lip with my tongue. I taste blood. He leans in and licks it, takes my lip between his, sucks hard while watching me. When he pulls back, I look down at my ripped dress, hear my own panting breath.

"Look at me," he commands.

I don't make a sound. I shake my head, the slightest shake.

"Cilla," it's a groan, a sound with an edge. A threat. And the squeezing of his hand is another warning.

I force my gaze to his, feel myself burn. I don't know what I expect. Gloating? Some rude, demeaning comment? More humiliation? But all he does is look at me like he's memorizing me, my face, my eyes, like he knows what I'm feeling. What I'm thinking. Like he sees right through me.

"You're mine, Cilla. See it when you clean my cum off your thighs. Remember it when your cunt throbs as you try to sleep tonight. Know it. And know that you loved it. That you came so hard you couldn't fucking stand when it was finished. And most importantly," he leans in even closer so his mouth is touching my ear, "know that I know."

He releases me and steps back and I can't stand so I slide down along the wall and he watches me. There's no pity in his eyes. No violence. Only a contentment, a victory. Because tonight, Killian Black won.

8

KILL

I'm driving back into the city. I still smell her on me. Feel her cum on my dick. She was so tight, I thought for a minute she was a fucking virgin. And she was aroused from minute one.

I meant what I said to her too. That I like taking. Thing is, she likes it too. She wants it. Wants me to take. She just can't bring herself to admit it. But her pussy, it doesn't lie. Her lips may lie, but her body can't.

My cellphone vibrates on the seat beside me. It's Hugo. I hit a button on the steering wheel and I can hear the club in the background.

"Kill."

His standard greeting. I met Hugo during my time behind bars. By the time I got there, he'd already served six years for killing some white supremacist prick. Back then, I wasn't sure of my release only four years into my sentence. But when Dominic Benedetti came through, when he pulled the strings that got me my early release, I hired Hugo as soon as he was out. Favors from the local boss of the Italian mafia don't come cheap and I needed him as much as he needed the work. I still don't know the details why Benedetti did it. I know he had some beef with my uncle, and I guess my killing him solved that, but he didn't owe me shit.

The gentlemen's club, Mea Culpa, it's mine. Not my big fucking dream, but it works. Makes me the money I need. Gives me a gateway to funnel through shit that, even though the local authorities know is getting funneled, needs to be done discreetly. They know their greedy little fingers are greased by the mob and they take it, all behind their hypocritical faces.

"We have a problem," Hugo continues.

I can guess what the problem is. His name is Benjamin Black III. My fucking dickhead cousin who, having no foot to stand on, still thinks he's owed something. And of all things, owed it by me. The only reason I don't kill the son of a bitch is because he's family.

Although I guess my uncle was family too, but that sick bastard deserved to die for what he did. He's the reason Ginny's in the ground. He's the reason I spent four years behind bars.

And I guess I do feel like I owe him my protection. The shit with his father—my uncle—happened when he was fourteen. He doesn't know the extent of what that prick did and, being the good guy I am, I wanted to spare him. But what's the expression? No good deed goes unpunished. That's about where I'm at with Ben, known to Hugo and me as Benji. But this stunt with Jones, it's going to need to be punished.

"What is it?"

"I want to bury my fist in your cousin's face, that's what."

"You and me both. I'm on my way in. Put him in a room to cool down. I need to talk to him anyway."

"It's different this time. He's brought friends to play."

"What are you talking about?" My cousin doesn't have friends.

"Antonino's men. Four of them. Benji's fucking walking around like he's the fucking king."

"You have got to be kidding me."

"Wish I were."

Arturo Antonino is the ousted boss of the Antonino family. In my humble opinion, Dominic Benedetti made a mistake letting him live after the incident with the Rossi family. He'd disappeared for a while, kept a very low profile, which was smart. But he's basically split the Antonino family in two, half of whom are loyal to his cousin, and in turn, loyal to the Benedetti family, the other half merged with the Rossi family. If Antonino thinks he can somehow beat Dominic Benedetti in his own territory, he's a fucking idiot with a death wish. Which makes my cousin, who I know for a fact is an idiot, another idiot with a death wish.

"I can ask them to leave but it's exactly what they want me to do. There's a van parked outside that I have a feeling is full of Rossi soldiers."

"I'm about twenty minutes away. Just keep an eye on Benji. The fucking imbecile."

"You got it."

I'm parked in my reserved spot at the club fifteen minutes later. The lot is full, but it's always full, and I see the van Hugo mentioned he thinks contains Rossi soldiers. It's sitting at the farthest corner of the lot with the back doors open. I don't know how many men there are but it's more than the two standing outside smoking, watching me. They've also busted the overhead streetlamp. Fuckers.

The club itself is located inside a large warehouse where the main floor is the club, the basement is, well, where some of the uglier business gets handled. My office is on the floor above and Hugo lives on the top level.

Two men stand sentry at the large doors of the front entrance. They're the first checkpoint. I nod to their greeting and they pull the doors open where inside is the second checkpoint.

"Hey boss," Chrissy's thick voice greets me. Chrissy is actually Chris, a transgender who may look like a sweet piece from behind the glass wall, but if you fuck with her, you'll be on your back with the spiked heel of a $500 pump impaled in your throat. Met her in prison too. She was Chris then and got the shit beat out of her regularly. At least until I showed up she did. It only made her stronger, she says. Cup half full person, I guess.

"Evening, Chrissy. I hear we have some unwanted guests." I strip off my coat and hand it to the girl working coat check tonight.

The smile she reserves for the usual clients vanishes. "Rossi bastards. I know for a fact at least one is armed. I let Hugo know right away."

"You did the right thing. I'll take care of it."

Two more men stand at the second set of doors that lead into the club itself. They open both when I approach and I survey the space, spotting Benji immediately. He and his new friends are at the far stage where two girls are putting on a show. Bills carpet the floor of the stage, which I can understand is a huge motivator. I pay my girls well, but it's the tips that take them into the six-figure earning category.

Benji doesn't see my approach, but two of the men around him do. I notice their shiny revolvers when they pull their jackets back. Hugo flanks me as I give them the once over. They should know better than to come into my club armed. Benji should know better.

I walk between the men like I don't give a fuck, because I don't, and wrap an arm around Benji's shoulders just as he realizes I'm there.

"Ben, Ben, Ben," I say, looking down at him. He stumbles to his feet. All 5'8" of him. At 6'4", I've got eight inches on him. And about fifty pounds of solid muscle.

"Kill," he says, his bloodshot eyes always betraying that little momentary panic he feels in my presence. He shrugs free of my hold and clears his throat, straightening his spine. He looks an inch taller tonight. I look down at his feet and I chuckle. I have to. The douche is wearing what must be a specially made pair of men's shoes with a fucking platform. "You need to teach your dog there some manners," he says, pointing to Hugo. He picks up his drink, some mixed shit, and takes a long sip from the straw. A fucking straw.

I feel Hugo's eyes narrow beside me and see how Ben shrinks back. Jesus. What a fucking pussy. How the hell do we share blood?

"You know you're welcome here anytime you like, but that invitation doesn't extend to members of either the Antonino or the Rossi families. Don't tell me you didn't know that."

"They're my friends."

"Don't be an idiot." I'm not fucking around. I don't want trouble, not inside. "You also know my rule about weapons."

"We're just having some fun. Spending money in *your* establishment. Putting money in *your* pocket."

"I don't need their money. Time for your friends to go home. You and me though? We need to have a talk."

He rubs his eye, his nose, as he looks around nervously. I wonder if he's not high on top of being drunk.

I look at Hugo. "Have Chrissy call my cousin a cab. Boys," I say, turning to the men surrounding Ben. My men circle them. "Time to go home. And you tell whoever it is who ordered armed soldiers on my property I better never learn his fucking name. Understand?"

The idiots stand there looking at Ben for direction and he's still rubbing his nose, one eye on the girls still making out on the stage.

"Get them out of here," I say.

My men surround them, disarm them in a matter of moments, and have them out the exit before the rest of the patrons even notice what's what. Ben sits back down and returns his attention to the girls. I take a seat beside him.

"What was that stunt with Jones?" I ask.

"What stunt?" But he knows what I'm talking about.

I take a deep breath in, then out. I turn to him. "Look at me, Benji."

"Don't fucking call me that." He's struggling to drag his gaze from the women.

"Then grow the fuck up and I won't have to."

He faces me.

"Why would you have an idiot like Jones steal from me? You knew he'd get caught."

Ben's eyes harden. "It's fucked up when people you trust fuck you, isn't it?"

He's trying to make a point but he's doing it badly. "I don't trust him. I never did."

Ben gives me a nervous giggle. "Just keeping you on your toes, Cous. Come on, just messin' with you. You know I'm loyal to you."

"You're not messing with me. You're messing with the fucking mob if you steal their coke. Do you have any idea what they'll do to a guy like you?"

He clearly hasn't thought about that part.

"Let me put it in simple terms. If they leave you alive,

and that's a big if, you'll wish they hadn't. You don't fuck with men like Dominic Benedetti."

"There's a war brewing. New players in town. You don't know everything, Cous."

"I know your new friends will only get you in trouble. I thought you were smarter than that."

Ben turns his attention back to the girls on the stage and picks up his drink. He sucks back the rest of it, then turns to me. "Don't pretend you care about me, Kill. Not after what happened. What you did."

"You know why it happened." I stand. "We're not talking about this." I lean down close to him, take him by the collar, raise him up out of his seat. "I just need you to know that if you try to fuck me, you will fail. But when I fuck you back, I won't. Am I clear?"

I hear him swallow. He's scared. He always has been.

"Am I fucking clear?"

"Yes. Clear as a fucking bell."

"Good."

I release him and he sits back down. He returns his attention to the girls. I shake my head and head to the elevator. Hugo follows after instructing two men to keep an eye on Benji. We ride up to my office.

"If word gets to Dominic that Rossi's men were here, he'll send a message," I say.

"And you're afraid your cousin will get caught in that net?"

"Yeah."

"You don't owe Benji shit."

"I know that. I just feel sorry for the kid."

"He's not a kid anymore. He was before, but you took care of him. Your job is done."

"Because of me he's on his own."

"No, because of his father, he's on his own. He's bad news, Kill."

"What do you want me to do? He's my fucking cousin."

"He's a bad seed."

"You think I don't know that?"

"If Dominic finds out from someone else, he'll be wondering why you weren't the one to tell him."

The elevator doors slide open to my office. Once inside, I switch on the monitors and locate Ben in one. I keep one camera trained on him and switch another one on to show me what's happening at the Rockcliffe House. "I'll talk to Dominic," I say to Hugo.

He watches her over my shoulder. Cilla's in her bedroom, sitting on the bed, combing out her wet hair. Her face is serious, her eyes far away.

"What's the girl to you?"

"Piece of ass."

"Nah. More than that. Piece of ass you got plenty."

"I don't know. Different kind of ass."

He chuckles. "I'll go back to the floor."

I barely hear him. I've got my eyes locked on Cilla as she stands, strips off her towel and walks into the closet. When she returns, she's wearing a tank top and a pair of panties. She climbs into bed and switches off the light. I can still see her face. Night vision lens. She's lying on her back looking straight up into one of the cameras. It's like she's looking right at me.

I wonder about what Hugo said. *"What's the girl to you?"* I have no fucking clue.

Cilla slides one arm beneath the duvet and I know the instant her fingers find her clit. My dick gets hard as I watch her, her hand shifting the blanket as she spreads her legs and rubs herself beneath it. But it's her face I'm more interested in. She's got her eyes closed and she's caught her lower lip between her teeth. I reach to turn up the volume on that camera and I feel like the cost of the ultra-sensitive microphone has justified itself when I hear her quick breaths of air, her tiny gasps. Hear her make that sound when she comes, the one she made when my dick was splitting her in two. I rub my erection over my pants. I don't want to use my hand tonight. I want her. I want her slick, tight pussy. Want her heat, her warmth. I want to fuck her again. Make her touch herself again while I watch. Make her come again.

"What's the girl to you?"

Cilla draws her hand out from beneath the covers, rolls over onto her side and closes her eyes, this time to sleep.

Dirty girl. Doesn't even wash her hands.

"What's the girl to you?"

I don't fucking know. A distraction? Why did I take her to Rockcliffe House? Why did I open the house again? I haven't been there once since Ginny. Since my uncle. I always knew I'd have to go back. To face the past. Face my failing. Answer to the ghost of my sister.

Too many ghosts in that house. Hell, everyone's a ghost but me.

9

CILLA

I wake up to sunshine pouring in from the bedroom windows. I hadn't closed the curtains and after so many consecutive days of rain, I turn my face toward the bright light and, despite everything, it makes me smile.

At least for a minute until I move and am reminded of the night before by the soreness between my legs.

I sit up, drawing the blankets to my chest and remember how, after dragging myself to my feet and out of the library, I'd hurried up the stairs when I'd heard Helen moving around in the dining room. Shame had burned my face and I couldn't imagine anyone seeing me in that state. I'd wanted to lock the door but there wasn't a lock on it. At least not from the inside. I noticed, however, that while I'd been out of the room, someone had installed a sturdy latch to the outside. Nice.

But after all of that, after the fucking, the humiliation of coming, after scrubbing my skin raw, I'd lain in bed and, at the memory of Kill fucking me, I'd slid my hand between my legs and made myself come again.

I push the covers back to get out of bed, and go into the

bathroom to shower again. As if I could wash away the shame I feel. I don't look in the trash can where the heap of soft violet silk lies. The ruins of the dress. Like the ruins of my dignity. Is this what he wants from me?

After the shower, I go directly into the closet and choose a pair of jeans, a sweater and a pair of boots. At least I have my own bedroom. At least I'm not expected to sleep in his bed. I go to the door, half expecting it to be locked, but it opens and there's no guard outside. He gave me the rules yesterday. My room, kitchen and library. I guess he's testing me so he can have that opportunity to show me how he'll punish me.

Not yet, Killian Black. I won't give you that satisfaction yet.

I head down the stairs and into the dining room. I want coffee. And I want to go outside. Sit in the sun, even if the temperatures are freezing. Helen must hear me because she comes through the door carrying a silver coffee pot and wearing a smile.

"Good morning, Miss," she says.

It feels strange that she'd call me Miss but I leave it alone. I make myself remember she's part of this, of his world. She's not my friend.

"Good morning. Where's Kill?" I clear my throat. "Killian." To say his name feels so strange, especially the abbreviated version of it.

"He's not back yet, but he did send a package for you. Would you like me to get it now or after breakfast?"

"A package?"

"Yes, Miss."

I shake my head, eye the pot of coffee. "Now, please, and some coffee?" I wonder about Kill not being back yet. Does that mean he went out last night? After what happened in the library?

She nods and pours coffee into an elegant cup. The table is set for breakfast for one.

"Would you like something warm to eat?" she asks.

I see the toast on the table and shake my head. "No, this is fine. And I..." this feels so weird, like I'm asking freaking permission. "I want to go outside."

"After your breakfast, I'll call someone to take you."

So she knows I'm a prisoner. She knows the rules he set for me. She'll probably report back to Kill. "Thanks." I don't mean it.

I sip the coffee and butter a piece of toast. A few minutes later, one of the girls from the night before enters carrying a large-ish box. She sets it on the table and leaves.

Setting my toast down, I look at it. Read the return address. It's from the Apple store. I open the package and inside, I find a brand-new laptop. Suspicious, I pick up the envelope on top and open the flap to read the note.

You earned this last night.

Rage boils in my gut.

Fuck. You. Killian. Black.

I slap the note back in the box and stand, close the lid and call Helen. I'm fuming.

"Yes, Miss? Changed your mind about breakfast?"

"No. Here. You can throw this away."

I shove the box at her. She doesn't take it at first, but I push and she extends her arms.

"Miss?"

"In the trash, Helen. Right away." I'm fuming and walk out of the room, try the front door only to find it locked. I look around, not sure where to go, what to do. I don't want to go back to my bedroom. I'm too angry. But I saw a pair of sneakers in my closet earlier, and some running clothes. I head up and change into them and go back downstairs. This time I don't wait for Helen to come to the dining room. Instead, I walk into the kitchen.

She's startled but I don't care.

"I want to go for a run. Now."

"Of course." If she's offended by my rudeness, she doesn't let on. Instead, she picks up a phone and a moment later, there's a man at the kitchen door. My babysitter, I guess.

"Keep up," I snap, running past him and jogging around the terrace, past the swimming pool and into the wet, knee deep grass. I'm heading into the woods. I need to run, burn off some of this anger, because when Kill gets home, I need to be in control of myself. Because I'm going to tell him what I think of him and his stupid gift. I'm going to tell him where he can shove it. He thinks I'm some whore? That I fuck for money? For things? He can go fuck himself.

10

KILL

As if I don't have enough on my mind, when I walk into Rockcliffe House, I see the laptop sitting on the kitchen table and from the look on Helen's face, it's not good.

"What?" I ask, opening the lid of the box which isn't closed fully.

"She didn't want it, Killian," Helen says, turning her attention to the dishes.

The note inside is out of its envelope. I know exactly why she didn't want it.

"Helen."

She switches off the water and faces me, drying her hands on her apron. "Yes?"

"The girls can wash the dishes. That's why they're here."

"I don't mind."

"I want them to do it. Not you." She's too old to work so hard.

"Okay, Killian."

"Where's Cilla?"

"In her room. She went for a run earlier and after taking a few books from the library, has been in the bedroom."

"Did she eat anything today?"

"Exactly one bite of toast. She got very upset when she read the note," she says, eyeing the box. "She seems like a nice girl, Killian—"

"It's not that kind of relationship, Helen." I open the fridge, grab a beer and twist off the cap. My back is to Helen.

"You don't have to isolate everyone, you know," she says.

I don't respond. Helen's known me for as long as I can remember. She practically raised me and Ginny.

"Be gentler with her. She's scared," she continues.

I close the fridge and face her. "She should be scared." I pick up the box containing the laptop and walk out of the kitchen, draining half the bottle and setting it on the dining room table before going up the stairs to Cilla's room. I don't need this right now. Today has been a shit storm. She's here for stress relief. Time she learned her place.

Not bothering to knock, I enter her room.

Cilla's pulled a chair up to the window so her face is in the waning sun. She startles, drops her book as she stands.

"Knocking is polite," she says after clearing her throat.

"It's my house." I go in and drop the box on her bed.

"It's my bedroom for the next month."

I go to her, but force myself to take slow, steady steps. I need to keep a tight leash on the anger she manages to bring up in me. She must see it because she backs up a little, although there's not much space to retreat. She puts a hand on the back of the chair.

"Nothing is *yours*. Everything is *mine*."

"Including me. I know. Did anyone ever tell you you're like the bully on the playground?"

I stop a few feet from her. "Maybe I like being the bully."

"You would."

"I gave you a computer."

"As payment for fucking you."

"You said you need one for work."

"I just wanted mine. I don't need a brand new laptop, especially not when it's in exchange for...that. I'm not a whore. I don't need your money. We made a deal but that didn't mean I gave you permission to treat me like a prostitute."

"Permission?" I feel my eyebrows rise. "You needed to give me permission?"

She bends to pick up the fallen book, moves to the side, putting more space between us. I close it, back her into the wall, cage her in with my hands on either side of her head.

"I don't remember asking permission being part of our deal."

Emerald eyes stare at me. Her thick, dark bangs come to her eyebrows and only make the green seem starker by contrast. Her mouth is open and I see where I bit it yesterday. Tasted her blood. I touch my tongue to the tear on my own lip where she did the same to me.

"What's the girl to you?" Hugo's voice repeats in my head.

Maybe she's my match.

My gaze drops to her chest where the V-neck sweater leaves her flesh bared. She's wearing black and her hair's down. I touch the softly curling strand that rests on her breast, then tuck it behind her ear. Her breathing changes, comes shorter, then stops altogether. She stands perfectly still and I feel her watching me even as my gaze hovers over her lips, the curve of her collarbone, the smoothness of her skin. I touch the necklace she's wearing. She's had it on since the first night. It's a fine gold chain with a small cross hanging from it. I take the cross in my hand.

"Jesus won't save you, you know," I say, not looking at her, studying the cross instead. Ginny had one like it. Trapped beneath the rope, the cross had embedded itself into her skin when she'd hanged herself. I remember feeling the divot in her skin after I'd cut her down, torn the noose from her neck.

I remember feeling how her neck had broken. How her head lolled to the side when I laid it on my lap. I hoped it had happened fast, at least. Hope she hadn't suffered.

No, that's bullshit. She'd suffered long enough to do that.

I close my eyes, my head is bowed so Cilla can't see my face. I don't realize I'm squeezing until I feel the chain break, until I hear her gasp. I don't look up. Instead, I close my fist over the little figure of Jesus on his cross and steel myself, forcing those images away, burying those memories deep in my gut. Willing myself to not see the chair she'd used lying on its side, not see her shoe on the floor beneath her, in a puddle of piss dotted with red. Not to see the blood on the insides of her thighs, the ripped sheets of skin.

I step back, turn away from Cilla, my hands on my face, my eyes, rubbing away the pictures that haunt me every day, every night.

"Dinner's at eight. Be dressed and at the table." I force the words out, my voice sounding strange, haunted.

On the verge of a break.

I walk out of her room without turning back, head to my master suite at the end of the hall. Inside, I strip off my clothes, change into running gear, head back downstairs and out the back door. From there, I run. I run hard, not caring that the ground is still soaked after too many days of rain, not caring that darkness has descended and that the woods will be pitch black. Not caring about anything at all but the exertion, the exhaustion of muscle, the pain which is the only thing that can force away those images.

It was like that in prison too. That's when I got so big. I lifted weights. I ran. I fought. Fuck, I raged. Pain is my Prozac. It's the only thing that keeps the demons at bay. Without it, rage will take over. And it will level everything, leave a wasteland behind.

It will decimate me.

Cilla steps out of her bedroom at 7:59PM. It's the same moment I exit mine. She stops dead when she sees me, presses her back into her closed door. I'm not sure if she's aware her hand is touching her neck, the place where her necklace once was.

I smile. I almost want to say it's to reassure her. Let her know I'm not going to hurt her. But the look I get makes me think I look like I'm baring my teeth in warning. I literally just ripped her necklace from her throat. I scare the shit out of her. It's what I want, right? It's what I told Helen earlier. So why do I feel like a shit?

"You look nice," I say awkwardly when I reach her.

She's wearing a knee-length black dress, this one with long sleeves. Her hair's pulled up into a tight bun and her bangs pinned back.

"Thank you," she says, her voice cautious, eyes never leaving mine like she's searching, trying to figure out which version of me this is.

"Shall we?" I gesture to the stairs. She looks down and nods, turns to walk ahead of me. The dress plunges low and I suck in a breath at the sight of her naked back, the curve of her spine.

She shudders, hugs her arms around herself. She stops, I almost collide into her when she turns. "I should get a sweater."

I shake my head, touch the flat of my hand to her lower back. A little shock sparks at the contact of flesh to flesh. I turn her. "I like you like this," I say, feeling like a Neanderthal.

Her eyes search mine and I wonder what she sees. A monster, perhaps. A beast she fears. That thought equally draws and repels me. Silently, she nods, turns and we go down the stairs and into the dining room.

Throughout dinner, she's cautiously quiet, watching me, eating her meal without a word. Drinking the wine I pour. The only sound is that of clinking silverware as we eat in silence. I know she has a hundred questions. A thousand. But she's smart enough not to ask them.

When we're finished eating, I set my napkin down and we stand. She follows my lead and I notice how she isn't quite sure what to do with her hands. I gesture for her to walk ahead of me and she knows where to go. She doesn't glance back as she makes her way to the library where I open the door and we enter.

"Sit down." Like the night before, I pour us each a drink, hand her a glass.

"Thank you for the computer," she says.

I'm not expecting that, but I nod in acceptance.

"Why do you want me here?" she asks right away.

"You asked me the same thing last night."

"I still don't understand."

"Why did you offer yourself?" I ask. Same as last night. I guess we're both on repeat.

She shakes her head. She won't answer.

I slide one hand into my pocket, search her eyes.

"Do I scare you, Cilla?"

She shakes her head, but the way her throat works when she swallows, the way her eyes widen, it tells me I do.

"You're a liar," I say. I swallow my drink, set the glass down and kneel on the floor before her chair.

Startled, she sits up straighter, her free hand grips the arm of the chair. I put my hands on her closed knees and push them apart. She makes a sound, and the ice in her glass clinks when she sets it down. I can't see her expression because I'm not looking at her face as I push the dress up, draw her toward the edge of the chair. I hold her legs wide, exposing her inch by inch until her pussy comes into view.

My hands squeeze her thighs. I study the wet, pink mouth of her sex, draw her folds open with my thumbs and bring my face to her, my nose to her, my mouth to her. I inhale deeply, her scent an aphrodisiac. She swallows audibly and her fingernails are digging into the arms of the chair. And when I sweep my tongue over her clit, she gasps.

I have never enjoyed eating a woman like I do Cilla. After that first taste, I devour her, tasting every inch of her, dipping my tongue inside her, taking her swollen clit into my mouth and sucking. I watch her face when I do, feeling her hands lock around my head, pulling me to her and pushing me away at once, and it's not long before she throws her head back, giving herself to it, to the pleasure, to me, coming on my tongue, her taste the most delicious taste.

When I'm finished, I stand. I wipe my mouth with the back of my hand as Cilla watches me, her breathing short, her face flushed. The shoulder of her dress has slipped, exposing one breast. I reach down, take hold of the dress and push it to her waist so she's sitting with her pussy and her tits exposed.

"Hands and knees," I say, pointing to the floor at my feet.

She doesn't move, just sits staring up at me. I bring my hand to her face, touch her cheek, twist it around to the back of her head and urge her down.

"Hands and knees," I repeat as she slides to the floor, but doesn't quite get into the position. She remains kneeling there, looking up at me.

I strip off my jacket and open my shirt. I don't have time to undress. I walk around her, kneel behind her. She doesn't look back. I slide her dress up her back and when it's at her neck, I push her head to the floor. She lowers herself onto her elbows, her forehead on the carpet. I undo my pants, widen her knees with my own as I take my position behind her. I settle in, take her hips in my hands, spread her wide, and I look at her. I just look at her for a long time. Her back is arched, her cunt is dripping. When I close my thumb over her tight little asshole, she gasps, clenches. I slap her hip.

"This is mine too. I want to see what's mine. Touch it. Fuck it." My voice is a low, deep growl. She cranes her neck to look behind her. "Mine, Cilla."

She swallows, faces forward. I wonder if she's preparing herself to be fucked in the ass, but that's not the hole I want tonight. Still, I close my finger over it, push a little, only because I can. Because I want her to know I own her. I own this hole. I own every part of her.

She makes a sound, but I see how her pussy is leaking down her thigh. I guide my cock toward her wet cunt, take my time tonight, watch her stretch to take me. She's tight, so fucking tight, and I know from the sounds she's making it hurts her, but I also know that pain will only intensify her pleasure. Intensify mine.

I push deep into her, taking in a breath, closing my eyes as her warmth engulfs me, resting here for one moment before pulling out to fuck her. I watch my cock disappear into her folds, hear the sounds she makes when I do, feel myself thicken inside her, until, finally, I bury myself in her, gripping her hard, her throbbing walls milking my cock, taking everything I give, everything I have.

I slump backward, my back to the chair. Cilla pulls away, draws her dress up over her shoulders, down over her hips as she stumbles to her feet, her hair out of it's neat bun, now looking like she's just been thoroughly fucked.

She's watching me with a look on her face I can't quite figure out, can't quite look away from.

"Am I getting another computer tomorrow?" she asks, pushing the shoulder of the dress that keeps sliding down her arm back up.

I rise, closing my pants as I do.

"Or something else?" She takes a step backward, and I realize she's now barefoot. I don't know why that strikes me. She looks around like she's thinking. "Maybe a car? I don't know. I mean, what's next when you start with a laptop?"

I chuckle, make my way to the liquor cart.

"It's funny to you, isn't it? I'm funny to you."

I pour a whiskey into a new glass, cap the bottle and take my time turning to her, the crystal tumbler in my hand. Studying her, I sip. Swallow. Feel it burn my throat.

"Is my cum sliding down your thighs?" I ask.

After everything, she's not expecting that. She shifts her gaze, her eyes glisten like she's on the verge of tears. I don't need tears though. I don't want them. She's here for one thing and one thing alone. I have to remember that.

"I hate you," she finally says.

"You've told me that already."

She walks to the door, puts her hand on the knob, turns it.

"Cilla." It's a quiet command to stop.

She does but doesn't turn to face me.

"You're not excused."

She stands there, clearly unsure what to do. How far to push me. So I push her instead.

"I need you to get back on your knees and clean my dick."

Tears have wet the skin around her eyes when she slowly turns her face to me. I watch her. I sip my drink. I'm an asshole, I know. But I can't be anything else. She can't be anything else than the thing I brought her here to be.

"Clean your own fucking dick, Killian Black."

With that, she pulls the door open and rushes from the library and I laugh. I laugh so hard, I double over with it. So fucking hard, I almost spit the whiskey out of my mouth. But when I stop, it's finished.

I look out into the hallway and wish I could hear her thoughts right now because she's running for her life. I go to the door, close it. I then take the bottle of whiskey and sit in the seat she was just in. Her shoes are on the carpet, and the room smells of sex. I leave the glass and drink straight from the bottle. Because I won't go after her tonight. I won't punish her tonight.

This is good. What happened is good. Because it puts us firmly on our separate sides of the boxing ring, where we belong. We're not friends. We're not lovers. She is nothing to me and what happened this afternoon, that goddamned cross, it won't happen again. I won't lose control to those memories again. I won't ever let them own me again.

11

CILLA

After my shower, my skin is raw. I scrubbed so hard, it still burns. What was I trying to get off me? His touch? His scent? It would be easy if it was only that. But what I don't understand, what I can't make sense of, is what happens to me when he touches me.

I've never felt safe with anyone. I've never really needed anyone.

No, that's not true. I just pretended all my life that I was fine. That I could handle life. I didn't need human touch. Didn't need to be held. When I fucked, I chose who. A bar. A stranger. A one night stand. No names exchanged. No kissing. I used them and I always left first.

It was always a control thing. My vibrator typically gave me more pleasure than any of the men I was with. I just needed to know I didn't need it. Didn't need *them*. Anytime I felt weak or vulnerable, I went on the hunt.

With him, I don't understand. I don't get it. He's forced me here. The deal I made I made for my brother. We both know that. I'm Killian Black's captive. It's bullshit he says I can leave any time I want and we both know it. Hell, I'm not allowed anywhere but in three rooms of this massive house, and can't even walk outside without a goddamned chaperone.

But when he touches me, it's like my body comes alive. It craves his touch. His hands on me. His mouth. His cock inside me, splitting me in two.

When he knelt between my legs and opened me up, fuck, I can't even...I could have come from the look in his eyes alone. Then he put his mouth on me and I was lost.

I was his whore.

I *am* his whore.

Because after that, when he stood and wiped his mouth with the back of his hand and ordered me to the floor, I *wanted* to kneel. To bury my face in the carpet. But I also needed to be made to do it. And I guess in a way, that's where he's trustworthy. He will make me.

And this is exactly why he's dangerous. Because with him, I'm not in control.

I glance at the clock. It's a little after two in the morning. It's raining again, I hear it coming down hard against the windows. I throw the covers back and get up. I can't sleep. I want a drink.

I'm only wearing a tank top so I grab an oversized sweater and slide my arms in, cocoon myself inside it, only realizing my feet are bare when I step out of my room and into the hallway, which isn't carpeted but hardwood. I almost go back inside to grab a pair of socks because this house always seems to have a chill, but it's quiet and dark and I decide to go downstairs and just find a bottle of something to bring back to my room. I know where he keeps the liquor, obviously, and it's one of the rooms I'm allowed in.

I fume at that. I'm *allowed* in the library. Like I'm a child.

And like a meek, scared little thing, I *obey* his rules. That knowledge turns my stomach. When did I become a rule follower? When did I obey anyone? It's not something I'm used to, hasn't been for a long time. Not since Jones got us out of that house. Before that, I obeyed because it wasn't me who was punished when I didn't. It was Jones. Every time.

The memory is crippling. I stop halfway down the stairs and close my eyes, force it back into the closet of my shame. I keep my past there. The years between mom and dad's death and the day Jones turned eighteen. I wish I could obliterate that time from my head. Get amnesia or something. Although one thing those years and the ones following taught me were that I can put them away. I can shove them into the farthest corner of that room, close the door and lock it. It's just that the lock is flimsy and pieces of the past seem to creep through the unending cracks in the walls.

But at least I have that room. Those years broke Jones in a way I've never been able to put him back together again.

My feet don't make a sound as I walk down the fourteen steps. I glance around the dark space. One lamp is left on in the living room and although it's a dim one, it's enough to guide me. I make my way to the library, open the door quietly, although it appears to be dark. I can't imagine he's still in there, but I exhale in relief when I confirm. Leaving the door open so I don't have to switch on any lights, I go directly to the cart that contains bottle after bottle of high end booze. After a quick inventory, I decide on a bottle of vodka and a glass and turn to leave. It would be better over ice, but I can't risk that so I'll have it at room temperature. I'm just glad to have the liquor at all.

I close the door behind me and am heading to the stairs when I hear a sound. It's quiet, a door sliding open. My heart leaps to my throat and I spin around, expecting everyone to be in bed, expecting to be alone.

The rain is loud, it sounds like a flash flood out there. You never know how powerful those things are until you see one for yourself. See it hurtling boulders and trees like they're nothing.

That's all I can think of as I watch him coming in from the sliding glass doors that lead to the back of the property. He's soaking wet, still dressed in the same button-down shirt and pants he'd had on earlier. Except he's not wearing shoes. He's in his socks, and they and his pants are covered in mud. He's making a mess as he takes three steps inside, sees me, stops.

He sways on his feet and rain is coming into the house, making the marble floor shine. I grip the neck of the bottle with one hand, the crystal tumbler in the other. He looks me over, eyes the bottle, and I notice the flashlight he's holding in his hand. It's like he only just realizes the door's open behind him and turns to close it. He's drunk, I know he is. And if I were smart, I'd take this moment to disappear up the stairs and into my room like I hadn't been here at all, but I'm not that smart, so I continue to stand there until he turns around to face me again.

"It's late," he mutters, his voice a low, deep grumble. "What are you doing?"

"I couldn't sleep." Where has he been this time of night? In this rain? "What are you doing?" I ask before I can stop myself. "Where are your shoes?"

He looks down like he's just realized he isn't wearing any, then looks up at me, and for a split second, I see something strange. Something familiar. Vulnerable. Like all of a sudden, he's a little kid. A lost little kid. But then he gives his head a shake, turns toward one of the closed doors of the house, digs into his pocket.

"Go to bed. Don't wander the house at night." He takes out a ring of keys.

"I'm not afraid of ghosts," I say to his back.

He stops, but doesn't turn. A moment later, I hear the key slide into the lock. "Maybe you should be." He goes into the dark room. Doesn't switch on a light. Doesn't close the door. If he closed the door, perhaps I would have gone up to bed, like he said. But he doesn't, and so I take a few steps toward it, curious about the room. Curious about him.

I step inside, my eyes adjusting to the darker room. I find him sitting on the leather couch, watch him bring a bottle of something to his lips. "You probably shouldn't drink any more tonight," I hazard, setting my own pilfered bottle and tumbler on the corner of the huge desk.

He looks up at me, his eyes bright and shining in the darkness, and purposefully takes another sip.

"Go to bed, Cilla."

I walk to him, I don't know why, but I do.

No, I know why. It's what I saw in his eyes a few minutes ago. It's like something in me recognizes it, recognizes that part of him. Feels somehow kindred to it.

I sit on the couch, not close enough to touch, and notice the muddy prints he's left on the animal hide area rug beneath my feet.

"Where were you?" I ask.

He turns to me. "You're a pain in the ass."

"So are you. Why were you outside without your shoes on? Without a coat?"

"What do you care?"

"I don't."

I look around at the dark walls. They seem to be papered

in black and a bookshelf lines two of them. Two windows draped with heavy curtains take up the one behind his chair and there's a painting I can't quite make out between them. A laptop sits on top of the desk, and next to it, a cell phone.

When I face him, he's watching me. "If you were smart, you'd run to your room, sweetheart."

Sweetheart. Again. It's disarming, but I shrug it off and study his eyes. "Would I be safe there?"

He thinks about this for a while before he finally replies. "No."

His single word answer is deliberate and it makes a chill run along my spine. He's being honest though. I think he's always been honest with me.

We sit like this for what seems like an eternity until he closes his eyes and leans his head back.

"Does it mean you believe in ghosts?" he asks, confusing me.

"What?"

He turns his head, meets my gaze. "You said earlier you're not afraid of ghosts. Does that mean you believe in them?"

"I...It's just something I said."

"You waste words."

I'm upset by this, by his disapproval. He rises to his feet and stands over me, waiting for me to do the same, I presume. I get up. He sweeps his arm toward the door and I go. The keys hang in the lock, and the door remains open as we go upstairs, him following close behind me. When I get to my room, I reach for the doorknob, but he puts his hand over mine. He's so close, I can smell him, the whiskey on his breath, the rain on his clothes, the man beneath. I turn my head a little. His is bowed, close, dark eyes burning into me.

"My room," he grunts. "Tonight, you'll sleep in my bed."

This makes my belly flutter, my heart race. Why? Why does he want me in his bed? Him fucking me is messing with me already. Why does he want me in his bed too?

"I don't..." I start, my voice breaking. "I don't sleep with anyone." I hear how ridiculous that sounds.

His eyebrows shoot up but he doesn't reply, instead, he pries my hand from the doorknob and we walk toward the double doors at the end of the hall. It's like a movie. Like the corridor is growing longer, the doors larger, the ones to his room looming like a dark omen. He's already fucked me. Why is this different?

Kill opens one of the two doors and hits a light switch. Two lamps on either side of the king size, four-poster bed come on and the room is bathed in golden light. The frame of the bed is steel, this room modern in comparison to the rest of the house. The carpet is lush and the tones are a deep, dark blue. The curtains are closed, as if someone already readied the room for sleep, and when I hear the door close behind me, I startle.

With a grunt, he points to the bed.

"Why?" I ask.

"Because there are ghosts, Cilla. Angry ones."

I'm watching him, trying to make sense of what he just said, but he turns and walks into the bathroom, leaving clumps of mud dropping from his clothes. A moment later, I hear the shower go on. I stand there like an idiot. I should do something. Find a weapon or a key or—no that's stupid. A weapon for what? To do what? A key to leave the house? When I go back on my word, he will hurt Jones. Period. One month. It's what I agreed to. To be his captive for thirty days. And that means he owns me.

With heavy legs, I walk to the bed. The shower switches off and I quickly duck beneath the covers, turning my back to the bathroom, trying not to think of how the sheets smell like him. I listen to him moving around the room, and a moment later the bed shifts under his weight. An arm wraps around my middle and I gasp when he draws me to him, turns me onto my back.

He's naked and although we've fucked, this is the first time I see his chest. Droplets of water cling to the muscles of his arms and shoulders, the hard ripples of his stomach. The tattoo on his chest, it's the Joker. And he's laughing and flipping someone off. Why do I get the feeling the joke's on him?

When I look up at Kill's face, I see that his eyes have cleared, the darkness softened a little, giving way to the specks of gold inside, vivid, intent on me, my face, on my eyes, my lips—skimming over my body. They lock on my panties. He pushes my sweater and tank top up a little, exposing my stomach. His fingers are feather light when he touches my belly button, trails a path to the waistband of my underwear. His eyes lock on my sex and I feel my body readying itself to betray me. Readying itself for him. Because I know what he wants. It's in his too bright eyes. His thick, ready cock.

His fingers slide beneath and he glances at me momentarily before returning his gaze to my sex and drawing my panties down, down, over my hips and thighs, off my feet. He brings them to his nose, watching me as he does this, as he inhales deeply with a satisfied moan. I feel my face burn when he tosses them aside, a knowing look in his eyes. He slides his knees between my legs and spreads them, and I feel his cock on me, on my thigh, my stomach. It leaves pre-cum in the places it touches. He takes my wrists, stretches my arms out to either side of me, holds them there and locks his eyes on mine when he penetrates.

I swallow, my back arching. He slides in easily—I'm slick for him—and I like it. I like that he's too big. That my body has to stretch to accommodate him. That it hurts to take him. I can give myself to this, right? For one month, I can let myself feel what this is. Whatever it is. This pain and the pleasure. If I choose it, doesn't that give me the power?

"Mine," he grunts, as if he's heard my thoughts.

He's moving slowly, taking his time, fucking me deep and with purpose, as if he'll brand me as his with this fucking.

"I like feeling your cunt stretch to take me. I like how tight you are. How ready for me. Always."

I bite my lip, he's hit that spot, just the right spot. I close my eyes. I can just feel now. I can just let myself feel this. It would be easy to lose myself in the sensation. I only have to take care I don't lose myself altogether.

"Open your eyes, Cilla."

He calls me back and I can do nothing buy obey. I want to see him like this, his big body over mine, his thick cock inside me. I can pretend I'm safe here beneath him. And I want to watch him, watch his face when he comes.

"I smell you before we fuck, you know. In the library too. You want this."

"I just want to come. Your dick will do for the next month."

He shakes his head, squeezes my wrists, slips his hands over mine, fingers intertwining, and I find myself gripping him back. Holding tight.

"No. You're not that simple, Cilla. Something happened to you. Something bad. It damaged you."

My chest tightens, my throat closes up and my eyes burn. He sees me and I can't hide from him, not now. Not when he's so close. Not when he's inside me.

"Just fuck me, Killian Black. Hard. Fuck me hard."

"No," he says, slowing down, moving his hips a little differently, making me feel every inch of him, like he'll take his time and know every inch of me.

It's too hard when he's looking at me like this. When I'm so vulnerable.

I don't want it to be this way.

I twist away, but he's got me pinned three ways and I can't get free. He smiles, like he knows what I'm trying to do. Like he knows what he said is true.

"You own my body. You have no stake over the rest of me."

"But I'm greedy. I want all of it." He draws my arms over head so they meet at the top of the bed, and lays his weight on me. He's moving faster inside me, his cock thicker. He's going to come soon. But I'm on the edge, closer than he is.

He wraps my hands around the cool steel frame of the bed and I grip tight as his fingers slide down over my arms, the sides of my body, my waist, my skin too sensitive to his touch. He never shifts his gaze as he grips my thighs, fingers digging into tender flesh as he pushes my legs up, forcing them to bend at the knee, opening me so his cock seems to penetrate to my core. Right to my heart.

I give over to sensation, unable not to, and he's fucking me hard now, not fast, but deeply, intentionally, like he's making good on his word. Like he'll take what he wants. He'll take all of it, all of me, inside and out, and I'm so fucking close, I can't resist, can't make the wave that's coming stop. I can't get a fucking grip.

A sound leaves my throat, my chest, it's a sigh and a sob and a moan of utter pleasure, of painful release, and I come. I come. And it's like I'm drowning. I'm out of air and all I can do is come.

"Cilla," he groans, and I realize I've closed my eyes. He lays his full weight on me and it's so wet between my legs and he's throbbing inside me, squeezing my hands again, too hard, too hard so they hurt, and my fingernails cut into my palms.

I can't breathe, he's so heavy. His eyes are closed and his face, oh God his face. I can watch his face like this for hours, days, and not get enough. Never enough. Because with him, it's like with no one else. Like nothing else.

And he is greedy. He will take it all. He'll take everything from me. Inside and out, he will own me. Destroy me. Decimate me. And when he's finished, there will be nothing left of me.

12

KILL

It's after ten in the morning when I wake up. I'm alone in the bed, but I knew I would be. Cilla slipped away a few hours ago.

Last night was the first time I slept next to a woman in a long time. Ever maybe. No one spends the night. Not me, not them. I fuck and I leave. Period. What she said about not sleeping with anyone, she meant that exactly. I've had Hugo look into her past. I know how she fucks. I know she's like a man in that regard. She goes to a bar called The Black Swan. I wouldn't set foot in it, personally. It's a shit hole. There, she picks up a guy, fucks him and walks away. She doesn't take anyone home, rents a hotel room in advance. I'm not even sure she bothers exchanging names.

When I made that comment about her being damaged, about something having happened to her, she confirmed what I suspected without words. The truth was in her eyes. She looked like someone desperate to escape. To make a run for it.

So later, when I felt her stir, I let her slide out from under my arm and disappear back into her own room. She can act like she's safe there. Like I don't know her secret. Pretend she's not as fucked up as I am.

But there's one thing I still don't know. Why did she do it? Why did she offer herself in exchange for her brother? She knew what I'd require. What I'd take. She had to know this would be different than what she's used to.

I turn my head, close my eyes again. Her scent lingers here, just beneath that of sex. I like watching Cilla come. It's like she gives everything up when she comes. Gives herself over completely. I want to think that's me. That she isn't like that with those other men.

The thought of them pisses me off and I throw off the covers and get up.

After a shower, I go downstairs to find the study door still ajar, my keys still in the lock. Helen comes around the corner and smiles.

"Good morning."

"Morning." I glance up the stairs and Helen seems to read my mind.

"She hasn't come downstairs yet."

I nod. "I'll just have coffee in the study."

"I'll bring it right away."

On my way in, I notice the mud's been cleaned up. After Cilla had left the library, I'd sat there with my bottle of whisky for too long. Although I didn't take a coat with me, I'd had my shoes on when I'd left the house and gone out into the woods. Gone to the barn on the edge of the property.

I close the study door and sit behind my desk, not bothering to open the curtains. I rub my face and take a deep breath in.

I hadn't been back to the barn since they took Ginny away. From the state of things last night, no one had. Maybe a mouse or two, but even the animals knew to stay away. Dust carpeted every surface, disturbed only by the weather blown in from the hole in one of the walls. Back when the house had first been built, it was a greenhouse, but by the time my family had moved in, it had been used more as a storage space. All I saw last night though was the chair she'd stood on as she'd slipped the noose around her neck. Saw her shoe. They hadn't taken that away when they'd taken everything else. The rope. The knife. A steak knife. She'd used that to try to cut out the baby.

Fuck.

I shake my head, clear the memory. The image of her trying to hide the pregnancy, trying to terminate it. The bloody mess on the floor. My baby sister all alone.

Fuck. I feel like I'm going to choke.

If she'd come to me, I could have helped her. If she'd come to me, she'd be alive today. God, she was fifteen. Fucking fifteen years old.

A knock at the door interrupts my thoughts. "Come in."

It's Helen and I find I'm disappointed. She sets the pot of coffee down, eyes the vodka and tumbler sitting on the edge of the desk.

"You can take those back to the library. I'm not to be disturbed for the next hour."

"Yes, sir."

She walks out and closes the door behind her. I pick up my cell phone and dial Dominic Benedetti's private line.

"Kill," Dominic sounds like he's just waking up.

"Morning, Dominic." We're business associates, not friends, exactly, but I do like the guy. He's a man of his word. "Something happened at the club last night I thought you should know about."

"What is it?"

"A few of Rossi's men were in there." I wait, but he doesn't speak. I can imagine his face though. He's always been a little hot under the collar, and I know he's pissed hearing this. "Nothing happened, but they did have a van full of soldiers parked outside."

"Antonino among them?"

"No. He's an idiot but not that much of an idiot."

Dominic chuckles. "Don't overestimate him."

"Listen, my cousin—" Dominic doesn't like Benji and the feeling is mutual. But still, he's my cousin. "You know he's not the sharpest tool in the shed." And I'm already covering for the bag of coke incident.

"Did that piece of shit bring them into Benedetti territory?"

I bite the bullet. "Yes. I took care of it and I don't think he'll do that again, but—"

"Fucking—how in hell are you two related?"

"I ask myself that all the time."

"The boy needs to learn a lesson, Kill."

"Let me handle it. If he pulls shit like this again, I'll teach it to him." And I will. Better to get his ass kicked by me than have his knee caps blown out by Dominic Benedetti.

"You know I respect you," he says. I know there's more so I don't speak. "But if you don't teach it, I will."

"Understood." Benji's safe, for now. "How's Gia?" I ask, changing the subject. "How many months along is she now?" I know exactly how far Gia Benedetti, Dominic's wife, is. And I know they struggled to get pregnant for two years so he's handling her with kid gloves.

"Five months and two weeks. It's a boy."

I hear the pride in his tone. And even though I know this isn't his first kid, I pretend like it is. "Congratulations. Pass that on to Gia, will you?"

"I will. Let me know when you talk to Ben."

"Will do."

After we hang up, I finish my coffee and get up. It's early, but I head to the club. I need to bury myself in work today. I need to do it to forget. I leave word with Helen that one of the boys should drive Cilla to the club tonight.

13

CILLA

A knock on my door rouses me from sleep. I sit up and rub my eyes, confused for a moment. Memories of the night before come flooding back. The knock comes again and I know it can't be Kill. He wouldn't knock.

"Cilla?" It's Helen.

"Come in." I glance at the clock. It's noon.

She opens the door and looks at me. She's carrying a tray of coffee and some food that she sets down. "Are you not feeling well?"

No, not really, but not in the way she thinks. "Just a little stomach ache," I lie.

"Do you want me to open the curtains?"

"No, thanks. I'll just sleep a little while." I don't want to run into Kill so I plan on hiding out in here as long as possible.

"I brought some toast," she starts.

"Thank you. Maybe later. Um...is Kill here?" I heard a car earlier and I'm hoping it was him leaving.

"No, he went to work. He said he'd send a driver to pick you up at nine o'clock this evening to take you into the city. You'll have dinner at the club."

"Why?"

"I don't know, dear."

"So he'll be gone all day?"

"Yes."

"Helen, can I ask you a question?"

"Of course."

"How often does he come here? To the house I mean? Does he spend weekends here or…" I trail off because I have a suspicion.

She looks straight at me. "It's his first time since his sister's death." I'm surprised at her honesty. And I guessed right.

"What time do I need to be ready to go?" I remember what she said, I'm just thinking.

"Nine o'clock."

"Okay. I'll just sleep a little longer and I'll be down later."

"All right." She pauses, sighs before she speaks. "He's not a bad person. He just comes off…"

"Like one."

She sucks in her lips. "I'll check in on you later," she says.

"No, I'm a light sleeper so probably best not to."

She studies me for a minute, then nods, turns and leaves. I wait until I hear her go downstairs before I throw the covers back and get up.

I have a feeling I know where Kill was last night. There's only one place he could have gone to. He'd been shaken up. Drunk too, but it wasn't that. He'd mentioned ghosts. Twice. Said they were angry.

I go into the closet and get dressed, choosing a pair of jeans, a sweater and flat boots. It's raining again, I can hear it on the window, so I anticipate mud.

I know what I'm going to do is wrong, but he didn't leave me a choice last night. It's like every time he touches me, he strips me bare. He reads me, sees me in a way I don't like being seen.

He knows I'm damaged. But he doesn't know why, because even if he digs, there's nothing to be found. No files, no charges, no accusations. Judge Callahan, the man who took Jones and I in, made sure of that. Just like he made sure neither of us would talk by promising my freedom when Jones turned eighteen if he kept his end of the bargain. A devil's bargain.

"A different sort of devil than Kill." I mutter the words aloud but I realize it's not true. Kill isn't like the judge. Not even close, even considering everything.

But that doesn't matter. I need to have leverage, something I can use to lay Kill bare, like he does me. I need to break him before he breaks me because what he said is true. He is greedy. And he won't be satisfied with just having my body. If this was ever about sex, that's changed. It's about owning me, body and soul. Hell, sex he can get anywhere. All he probably has to do is snap his fingers. What he's doing to me is something else, and I need to take back some control. To do that, I need to have something to hurt him with. And I know exactly what that something is.

Finding a raincoat, I slip it on and step out into the hallway. I noticed last night that the sliding glass door Kill came inside through doesn't use a key to lock it. Not from the inside at least. I creep down the stairs, keeping an eye out for Helen, but the coast is clear and I move quickly through the living room and to the glass doors. They're not even locked and I slide one open, step out, then close it behind me. A cold, fall wind gives me a chill as I glance around. It's creepy here, with the leaves of the half bare trees rotting on the damp earth, the furniture covered over, and the torn tarp over the pool constantly, unceasingly whipped by the wind. I hug my arms to myself, rub them for warmth, then sprint as quickly as I can into the woods. If I remember correctly, the barn is at the farthest point and it's an almost straight shot.

It's colder beneath the trees. The sun can't penetrate this dense forest. The ground is thick with mud and I think of him last night, trudging through this in socks. Was he even thinking? Was it a conscious decision? Or was he too drunk to think clearly? Too shaken up after seeing the place where she hanged herself. Because I know that's where he went.

Why had she done it? And how was it linked to the uncle's murder? I know it has to be. Too coincidental otherwise and if there's one thing I don't believe in, it's coincidence.

It takes me much longer than I expect to get to the barn because of the ground being so wet, but also because the property is much larger than it seemed on paper. When the greenhouse, which was built on the front of the barn, finally comes into view, it's much smaller than I expect. And for as well as the house has been maintained, this structure is the opposite. It's dilapidated.

Much of the glass that makes up the walls and ceiling of the greenhouse has been broken. I imagine it's due to time and disrepair rather than vandals. The property's gated. The back third—the original barn—is built of wood. I walk around it, look at the ground for proof that Kill was here last night, but find none. The rain would have washed it all away.

The door is literally hanging by its hinges and I carefully push it open. If I thought it was cold outside, it's frigid in here. I'm chilled the moment I step inside and hug my arms around myself, the creepiness of the place making me feel even colder.

It's dark too, the only light being the little bit that's coming in from the cracks between the planks of wood. I take a step in the direction of the greenhouse. Plants that never stopped growing have made this place into a dense jungle with green clinging to every surface, the smell of earth and mold overpowering. I can't walk in there if I want to, it's so overgrown.

But that's not the part I'm interested in anyway. I want to see the barn.

Wind whistles through the cracks in glass and wood and I look around for a light source, but remember that Kill was carrying a flashlight last night. I step toward the back, where it's darker, where the wooden roof has somehow remained mostly intact. Large beams support the structure and from one hangs a wire and from it, the broken remnants of a light bulb.

I walk deeper in while voices inside my head warn me to stop. To leave.

Tell me I have no business here.

Maybe they're not in my head at all, though, these voices. Maybe these are the ghosts Kill warned me against. The angry ones.

I walk on though, drawn to the darkness. I wonder which of the beams she used. I try to imagine the young girl walking from the house to this dilapidated old barn—was it dilapidated then? Try to think of her state of mind. Did she carry the rope with her from the main house? Was it night time? Daytime? Did she have second thoughts?

How scared was she?

Because I know she would have been afraid. Terrified.

What could lead a fifteen-year-old girl to hang herself? The papers never said, but she was a minor. That wasn't strange. Of course given what happened with the uncle, there was speculation. Some papers even painted Kill as the monster who pushed her to it. I don't believe that though. I just don't.

A noise behind me has me let out a small scream and I jump. A metal something crashing to the ground. But when I turn, there's no one there. Kill's not behind me. Neither is Helen. A ghost, maybe.

A moment later, a mouse scurries under the barn door, exiting this haunted place.

"Just a mouse, Cilla. Just a tiny, little mouse."

But my heart doesn't stop racing as I turn back to survey the space.

I look down. Mud does mark the places he was in here. And he was wearing his shoes from the look of the prints. I follow them deeper into darkness until I see it. See why he had no shoes on when he came back to the house. See the chair standing upright against one wall. It's been cleaned off because it's the only thing here that's not covered in a thick layer of dust. And what's underneath it—oh God—it's one of the saddest things I've ever seen.

I walk to it. To his shoes now caked in dried mud standing neatly against the wall. Between them a smaller shoe. A ballet flat.

With a shudder, I stare at it, noticing as I near it how the color has faded to palest pink. There's a smudge of the magenta it once was along the side. It's small, maybe a size six or seven at most. And between his giant ones, it looks like a young child's shoe.

I know it's Ginny's. And I know why it's here. There's only one reason. She must have had them on when she did it, and one must have slipped off or the cleaners somehow missed this second shoe.

I wonder how long he was here last night. What he did. I imagine what he feels or felt. I know how Jones was when it was me. I know what extent he went to in order to protect me. And I know how I feel every day when I realize over and over again that I couldn't protect him.

I wonder if that's Kill's hell. If that's his demon. The knowledge that he could not protect his baby sister. Because at least my brother is alive.

Lightning strikes in the distance, animating me. I turn and walk to the barn door, in a hurry to leave. To get out of this place where the past lingers. This space that ghosts haunt. It's a heavy place, like for the last few years air hasn't penetrated and everything has grown stale and weighted. When I set foot outside, I run. I run back to the house, suddenly feeling like I'm being chased, needing to go back to the land of the living.

This was wrong. I shouldn't have gone to the barn. Those warning voices were right. I had no business there. But it's too late now. I've seen it and you can't unsee what you've seen. It's not how things work. I know. My God, do I know.

I'm crying by the time I walk up the steps toward the pool and when I spy movement behind the glass doors, I don't try to hide. I'll take my medicine. And I do feel sick now, sick to my stomach.

I push the glass doors open and step inside, take off my mud-covered boots, and carry them up to my room. If Helen has seen me, she doesn't say a word, but in my room, I find the tray she'd left is gone, replaced by another with still warm tea and crackers. I strip off my wet clothes and climb back into the bed and close my eyes and when I sleep, all I can see are those shoes. Three of them. Lined up against the wall. A hangman's rope beside them, lying in a pool of blood and urine, a stained kitchen knife at its center.

14

KILL

I sit at a table in the restaurant of the club with a whiskey in front of me looking out on the floor. The restaurant part, which is small, is slightly elevated from the main floor where patrons can watch what's going on while having a meal.

This afternoon, I paid a visit to Cilla's brother. What happened last night has been bugging me all day. When I told her she was damaged she didn't deny it. She just looked at me like it was a fact, simple and straight. And I want to know what the damage is.

But Jones surprised me. When it came to talking about her, talking about their time in foster care, he was like a different person. He put up walls so thick and so high, they were impenetrable, even for me. Whatever happened to Cilla when she was a kid, he's not talking.

And something did happen.

The only house they spent a significant amount of time in was at Judge Herbert J. Callahan's. He and his wife took in foster kids for years. He's in his late seventies now. Retired.

I know people though. And the cleaner they look on the

outside, the dirtier they are on the inside. See, you have to watch out for men like the good Judge as much as you do men like me. They'll fuck you just like I will. They just may be more discreet about it.

Jones didn't give anything away. All he said was what I already knew. Parents were dead and since they had no other living relatives, they went into the foster care system. No one wants to adopt teenagers. And all there is on those years they spent with the Callahan's are two hospital reports, one of a broken arm and a second time a broken ankle. Cilla's. She'd fallen down the stairs is what Jones said. Twice.

That sounds way too fucking coincidental and I don't buy it. I don't even know if he wants me to.

But why in hell would he defend Judge Callahan if the old man abused her? Especially now that they're both adults and he can't touch them.

If that wasn't enough, I had a call from Helen informing me Cilla had snuck out of the house and when she'd returned she'd been soaked and covered in mud. It doesn't take a genius to know where she went.

When Hugo walks onto the main floor, I check my watch. It's almost ten o'clock. Cilla will be here soon. I want to know if he's learned anything.

The waitress walks over as Hugo takes a seat across from me.

"Usual?" she asks him.

"Yeah." He sets a file down on the table and slides it over to me. The look on his face tells me it's not good.

I open it, glance at the sheets inside, waiting while the waitress delivers Hugo's drink.

"A dirty judge," I say. I expected that.

"The dirtiest kind." He reaches over and flips a few

pages back. "These are the kids he took in. Always teens. Always a pair—brother and sister. Always an older brother, younger sister."

I like the sound of this less and less.

"They all stay two years. When the brother turns eighteen, he gets rid of both of them."

I look at Hugo, raise an eyebrow.

"Like in Jones and Cilla's case. Judge grants the brother custody. They disappear. But—" He flips a few sheets to a copy of a newspaper article. I check the date. It's from almost four years ago.

"This one didn't disappear. Her brother did, but she didn't. She claimed abuse when they lived in the Callahan home. Came forward because her brother committed suicide. Turned out he was a meth head and, given the Judge's impeccable reputation, she was played as some pariah out for money. But you know how I feel about judges and the system."

I know. Hugo spent too long in prison. He'll never feel any other way.

"Jones won't talk but something happened there," I say, closing the file. "Where's Callahan now?"

"Florida. Moved two years ago."

"How would you like to get out of this shit weather and get some Florida sun for a few days?"

Hugo grins, swallows his whiskey. "I'll leave first thing tomorrow morning."

"Thank you."

The front door opens then and John, the man I sent to bring Cilla, walks in. I feel Hugo's eyes on me when I stand and button my jacket as Cilla enters a moment later.

I clear my throat.

He clucks his tongue and gets to his feet. "I'll talk to you later, boss," Hugo says.

I don't take my eyes off her. "Later." She's still got her coat on so I can't see what she's wearing, but she's got on a pair of high-heeled black pumps. When John puts a hand at her back to guide her to the restaurant, she brushes it off. She spots me in the same instant and stops when our eyes meet. I wonder if it's guilt. If she knows I know what she did today.

She resumes walking. The eyes of other diners follow her when she climbs the two stairs to the restaurant and approaches me.

"Cilla," I say, drawing out her chair.

"Killian."

She doesn't like calling me Kill. "Take off your coat."

She looks down as if just realizing she still has it on. Unbuttoning it, she slips it off her shoulders. I take it and hand it to John. "Thank you, John."

"Sir."

He turns to walk away and I look Cilla over. She's wearing a strappy black dress that clings to her. The hem comes to mid-thigh and she looks stunning. I nod in approval and gesture for her to sit. She does and her gaze moves across the room and while it does, I take her in. She's left her hair loose and it drapes thick and dark down her back. Her heavy bangs frame her pretty eyes as she watches the dancers, three of them on three different stages. It's a classy place, one for the wealthiest of the wealthy, but ultimately it's a strip club. And she's not impressed.

I grin. "Not good enough for you?"

"Women taking their clothes off while men sip expensive drinks and stroke their dicks isn't impressive, no."

"Each of the women chooses to do this. Don't judge what you don't understand."

"I'm not judging. I just wouldn't want to be one of them."

"And that's fine for you, but I think you are judging."

"You don't know me."

"I know you better than you think."

She drops her gaze to her lap, laying her napkin on it.

"See that one there," I start, pointing to one of the dancers. "Her stage name is Brandy. She's got a two-year-old at home and is one year from graduating law school. That's Lola there, she works with high-risk kids, to keep them off the streets. Julie, well, she just likes having men watch her take her clothes off, and why not? She's a beautiful woman. She uses what she has to make a very decent life for herself. And she gets to keep all the control." From the look on Cilla's face, I've hit a nerve. "Like I said, don't judge what you don't understand."

"Like I said, I wasn't judging." She picks up the menu. "But you have to admit, there's a stigma that comes with the word stripper."

"Stigmas are created by closed-minded, pole-up-the-ass people to make themselves feel superior. Make up your own mind after you've got all your facts."

She sets the menu down and cocks her head to the side. "So did you bring me here to show me what a good guy you are? Hiring all these women to strip for you because they want to? To show me how because of you they *keep all the control*?"

I count to ten. This isn't how I want this evening to go. "I wanted to have dinner with you. And I thought you'd want to get away from Rockcliffe House for a night. That's why I brought you here. That's all."

That gives her pause. She lowers her lashes but doesn't quite apologize.

I signal for the waitress who brings over a bottle of wine from my private collection. Cilla's quiet while she pours.

"Do you know what you want to have to eat?" I ask her.

She looks up. "The filet mignon, well done, with roasted potatoes and a salad please."

"I'll have the same, but make my steak rare."

"Right away," the waitress says and leaves with our menus.

"You're hungry," I comment.

"Dinner's late."

"It's not your little adventure that worked up an appetite, is it?" I ask, wanting her to know that I know.

She flushes, blinks rapidly and looks around the room. "Where's the bathroom?" she asks, rising.

I nod in the direction of the lady's room. Her heels click as she walks away and I scan the patrons of the restaurant, making note of who's watching her, who's with whom, memorizing alliances. These are dangerous men. This is a dangerous world. And when Cilla returns to the table, I wonder for a moment why I've brought her here. In public. Because I know each of these men is, in turn, watching me. Taking inventory of what's mine.

We don't speak, but drink the wine instead. She's clearly anxious under my gaze, but I don't mind that. I like it, in fact.

When the waitress brings dinner, Cilla eats with gusto. I make a mental note to tell Helen to feed her regularly whether she asks for meals or not.

"What were you looking for?" I ask her.

She doesn't pretend to not know what I'm talking about and I respect her for that. She puts her fork down, chewing on a piece of meat as she considers her answer. "I wanted to know where you went," she finally says after swallowing.

"But you knew where I went."

She stares at me, uncertain what I mean, but perhaps suspecting.

"You wrote a piece on Rockcliffe House two years ago. You didn't use your full name when you published. You used Hawk instead. Why?"

She clearly didn't know I knew this, but I look into the background of every person I come in contact with. It's just I didn't expect to find what I did on her.

"That was a fluff piece. A ghost story. I want to be a serious writer."

"So you were looking for my sister's ghost out there?"

She chokes on the bite she just put into her mouth and gulps half her glass of water to wash it down.

"I don't like wasting words, Cilla. I already told you that."

"I wanted to know why you'd come back like you had last night. Barefoot but for your socks. It was strange. And you were drunk. I thought you were, at least."

"I was when I went out there."

"What happened to your face?" she asks. "The scar?"

I know what she's talking about. I pick up the bottle and refill her glass, then take a sip of mine, set my glass down and lean back in my chair before answering.

"That's the cut my uncle got in before I stuck a knife in his gut."

Her mouth falls open and her eyes go wide.

I grin. "It was a long time ago and he deserved it. Why do you look shocked? You know this already. It's not a secret. Everyone in this place knows what I did."

"Why did you get out of prison after only four years?"

"I served my time."

"No, you didn't. You only served four years."

I lean forward, pick up my last forkful of meat and stick it into my mouth, crushing the tender flesh between my teeth.

"My uncle deserved to die. I wasn't the only one who thought so." I wipe my mouth and set my napkin on my plate.

Cilla slumps back in her chair, picks up her glass and drinks the last of it. I signal to the waitress. "Get us another bottle."

"Yes, sir."

"What did he do?" Cilla asks, like she's barely realized the waitress was just here.

I study her for a very long time before replying with less emotion than I thought I could. "He'd been raping my sister for a long time. She was fifteen when she died."

Cilla's face goes white. That detail she didn't know. Not many people do. I don't know why I just told her.

I unclench my fist and rub my hand across my mouth.

Cilla is thoughtful for a long time. I don't anticipate her next question. I think it's going to be something else. Some words of pity. But she surprises me. She always seems to surprise me. "What does it feel like?" She's watching me so intently, I don't think she's blinking.

"What does what feel like?"

The look in her eyes, it's strange. Dark. Too dark for her.

The waitress comes to replace our empty bottle. I pour for us both and Cilla waits to speak until I'm sitting back again.

"Stabbing a man."

Our eyes are locked and I don't understand what I'm seeing. She's trembling a little, and her face is ashen, but there's something in her eyes, something desperate, something wild and vengeful. Something old and sad.

"Let's go," I say, standing up. I pick up the bottle and wait for her to stand.

It takes her a minute to move, to blink again. I pull her chair back and she rises. I take her arm and she doesn't resist when I lead her toward the elevator. When the man stationed there sees us coming, he pushes the button and the doors slide open when we reach it.

Suddenly, I feel like I need to hide her away. Like I shouldn't have had her out here, where everyone would see her. They'll want to know who she is. They'll look into who she is and I don't want them to. I don't want anyone to. I want to keep her hidden. Keep her to myself.

I don't let her go until we're in my office. The elevator doors close behind us and she walks toward my desk, drawn to the monitors there. There are six of them and currently, five are set on the club and one on the house. Helen is moving around the living room. Cilla watches her, cocks her head to the side as she does.

From the wet bar, I retrieve a wine glass and pour her one from the bottle I brought up. For myself, I pour a whiskey. She turns to look at me when I approach, takes the glass from my hand.

"You watch the house?"

I sip my drink and nod. I haven't thought about what it felt like to drive the knife into my uncle's belly for a long time, but I remember it. I remember breaking skin, cutting through fat. Muscle would give more resistance, but my uncle's gut, well, it easily yielded the pound of flesh I required.

I look Cilla over, look at how her nipples press against her dress. Watch how her hand trembles when she brings the glass to her lips, barely taking a sip as she watches me. I set my drink down and take my jacket off. She puts her glass next to mine. I turn her so she's facing the cameras, lean her forward, place her hands flat on the desk.

I draw her hips backward, raise the dress up along her thighs, over her hips, up her back. She's wearing panties. A lacy black pair. I draw them down to mid-thigh, look at her perfect ass. At her bent over like this. She's almost more naked for the underwear.

Raising my hand, I bring it down on her hip.

She gasps, spins around, hands on her ass. "What did you do that for?"

"I told you no panties."

She studies my eyes, doesn't battle me with words.

"Turn around, get your elbows down on the desk and be grateful I'm only punishing you for the panties."

She hesitates, but a moment later, does as she's told. I arrange the dress high on her back. The panties have slid to the floor and pool around her ankles. I raise my hand and slap her ass again. She grunts, but holds still while I continue spanking her. Ten times on each cheek. I know it stings from the way she wriggles around, and I have to lay a hand on her low back to keep her in position, but this is nothing to what I can do. Nothing to how I can punish her.

When I finish, I cup both reddened cheeks. They're warm. I rub the sting from them.

Cilla cranes her neck to look at me.

"Next time, I'll use my belt."

I can't read what's in her eyes but she swallows hard enough for me to hear. I lean over her and push a few buttons so the camera switches to the one in her room. When she turns to the screen, she recognizes the setting. I push another button to take us back to two nights ago.

"You watched me."

When I don't reply, she shifts her gaze to me.

"You watched me, you sick bastard."

"I like watching."

Slowly, I move to my knees behind her. The look in her eyes changes and she licks her lips.

I'm holding her thighs, I kiss her hip, draw my hands up to splay her open.

"Getting your ass spanked gets you wet, Cilla." She doesn't reply, only tenses up a little. "Are you wet like this for the others?" I ask, licking her once.

She sucks in a breath, arches her back.

"Are you?" I ask again, licking again, this time letting my tongue circle her asshole.

"No."

"Just for me." I glide my tongue over her pussy, then her tight little hole.

"Just...for you."

I kiss her pussy, her ass, lick her, dip my tongue inside her, taste her while I listen to her moans, her want, her desire. When she's close, I draw back, rise to my feet, one hand on her hip to keep her in place while I reach to the desk drawer with the other.

She watches me take out a small container of lube, watches me open it. The video on the screen starts over again, Cilla sliding her hand beneath the covers. Cilla rubbing her clit. Cilla making herself come. I turn the volume up before drawing her hips farther back. I pour lube onto her lower back so it drips a little down the cleft of her ass. I take that lube and begin to rub her asshole.

Cilla moans. She arches her back. "I want to hate you," she says.

I slide my thumb into her asshole and she lets out a deep sigh.

I say nothing. Instead, I undo my belt and pants, free my cock, grip it.

"Are you a virgin here?"

She nods.

I slide my cock into her pussy and draw my finger out of her ass, gather more lube onto two fingers and slide them into her tight hole.

She pulls away, gripping the edge of the desk. I draw her back toward me.

"Your ass belongs to me, Cilla. Be still now. I'm going to fuck it. I'm going to fill you up with cum and you're going to drip down your thighs when you take me."

"It hurts."

"The best things do."

I draw my fingers out and slide my cock, slippery with her juices, to her asshole. I rub the rest of the lube onto it, my eyes on her tiny little asshole as she waits obediently to take me. She's gripping the desk when I push the head of my cock against her ass.

She wriggles, lets out a groan of protest.

"Shh. Relax." I slide one hand around to her clit and begin to rub and when I do, she relaxes a little and I push, entering her slowly, taking my time, feeling her warm and tight around my cock as she stretches.

I begin to move, her clit between my thumb and forefinger, and I take a little more with every one of her moans.

"Kill—"

"Come, Cilla," I say when I'm about halfway in. I won't last long, she's so fucking tight.

She's an obedient girl when she wants to be and she

comes, laying her cheek on my desk, moaning, her fingers clawing at the oak, and I watch her and slide in deeper, pumping slowly in and out of her until I'm fully seated. I still there, for one moment savoring this, me inside her, her tight and warm and holding me. I only move again as she comes down from her climax, taking her clit between thumb and forefinger again. She's ultra-sensitive now and panting, begging me to stop, begging me for more. I fuck her harder, her passage opened to me, taking me and when she comes again and her walls throb around me, I thrust one last time and my cock pulses as I bury myself inside her, emptying inside her, filling her up, owning one more piece of her.

15

CILLA

Kill has barely pulled out of me when the elevator doors slide open and that horrible man, Hugo, walks in.

I gasp, straighten, try to cover myself, but my panties are at my feet and Kill's cum is dripping out of me.

Hugo stops, clears his throat, turns away. "Apologies."

Kill buttons his pants and wraps his hand around the back of my neck. "I didn't say you could get up."

"What?"

He pushes me back over the desk, pinning me to it with just a little pressure on my neck. That's all it takes to keep me down.

But when he raises my dress to expose me again, I cry out for him to stop. To let me up.

He leans over my back. "Stay. Down." My cheek is plastered to the cold wood of his desk and his face is so close to mine that I feel his breath on me. "Obey me, Cilla," he whispers his warning. "Or I'll whip your ass while Hugo watches."

I have no doubt he will. I blink, tears of shame burning my eyes. I close them, my acquiescence. He straightens.

"No problem, Hugo," Kill says and I feel him walk away. Neither Hugo nor I speak, but I hear water go on in what I assume is the bathroom.

I stay where I am. Bent over. Ass bared. Cum dripping down my thighs. Mine and his. And I hate myself for it. Because a moment ago, I told him I wanted to hate him. I wanted to. But I don't. I despise myself instead.

"What is it?" Kill asks, returning to the room.

"Benji's here."

"Alone?"

"Yeah. But he's drunk as a skunk."

"Fuck. Keep an eye on him. I'll be down in a minute."

I hear the elevator doors slide open, then close, and still I don't move. Ice clinks in a glass and I open my eyes to find Kill leaning against the bar watching me.

"Bathroom's through that door. Get cleaned up. Stay here, don't mess with any of the equipment and let that play." He gestures to the monitor that keeps repeating the image of me playing with myself, the sound turned up so I hear myself come over and over and over again. Hugo would have heard it too.

I'm humiliated. I straighten slowly, bend to pick up my panties, very aware by the soreness of exactly how I was penetrated. Of how he claimed another part of me.

Kill turns to the elevator where the doors slide open.

"Why did you do that?" I ask.

He doesn't turn around and doesn't answer my question. He says one word instead.

"Warm."

"What?"

"Warm. It feels warm. The blood. There's a lot of blood. I

cut into his stomach, carved out a pound of flesh. I weighed it to be precise."

"Oh my God." I'm going to be sick.

"That's why the papers called me a monster. A beast." He's silent and I wonder if he's reminiscing on this horrible act. "I did it so he'd bleed out slowly. Painfully. I stood and watched the life literally drain out of him." He pauses, meets my horrified gaze in the mirror. "I used the knife my sister used to cut out the bastard he put inside her."

I cover my mouth. He steps onto the elevator and turns to face me. "Get cleaned up and stay here until I'm back for you."

He doesn't wait for me to answer and the doors slide closed behind him.

My mind a blur, I go into the bathroom. It's fully equipped with a stand-up shower. I strip off my clothes and switch it on, wrapping my hair on top of my head, using a rubber band I find in one of the drawers to hold it in place. I wash myself, wash him off me, feel him still sliding out of me.

I'd never been fucked that way before. It requires giving up my power. Trusting the man doing the fucking. I've never come close to allowing anyone that kind of power over me. Kill, he took it. But I didn't fight him. Didn't fight it. I can tell myself it's part of the deal all I want, but I know that's not all there is to it. As much as I want to hate it, hate his domination, hate my submission, it turns me on. He makes me come like I have never come, not with a man, not with my fingers. He makes me come in a way that I lose myself.

Maybe I need those moments. Maybe I need to lose myself a little. But before that loss, I'm laid bare. It's like being skinned. Everything is exposed. Everything hurts. But then there's release. Is that why, in a way, I want this?

I shake my head, switch off the shower and grab a towel from the rack to dry off. The heat of the shower has fogged up the mirror so I wipe it with my hand.

My reflection is obscured in the steam but I stand looking at it, trying to recognize the woman looking back at me. It's weird to know your face and not really know it. To feel like a stranger in your own skin. I don't know who I am. It's been eight years since we left that house. Eight years since anything bad has happened to me. I want to say eight years since anything bad has happened to Jones, but I don't think that's accurate. I sometimes don't know if, even though he walked away, if he wasn't too broken already. If all these years, I've been lying to myself, trying to put on a front, unable to face the reality that he'll never be okay. Never be whole.

Maybe it's because I need to believe he is so that I can pretend to be whole myself.

And maybe I'm selfish to not let him go.

"Warm. It feels warm. The blood. There's a lot of blood. I cut into his stomach, carved out a pound of flesh. I weighed it to be precise."

I look down at my hands, clean, fingernails polished. I imagine the warmth of blood as it runs over them. As I plunge my hands into Judge Callahan's belly.

I want a pound of flesh. I want a hundred pounds of flesh. Two hundred. Enough to wipe away any trace of the man. Enough to erase history. To make me forget. To make Jones forget.

A tear drops onto my palm and my head snaps up. I take a deep breath in, fix my features, harden my face. I get dressed and walk back into Kill's office. Without hesitation, I pick up the glass of whiskey he left behind and swallow it, then pour myself another and do the same before pouring a third. I sit on the couch for a long time watching the images on the various screens but not seeing anything. I drink.

I have to force myself to stand. To walk to his desk, carrying both bottle and glass with me. I'm alone and I need to take advantage of that. I drink a little more. Refill my glass. I want to smash the bottle against the screens. I can't stand it anymore, seeing myself, hearing myself. But instead, I switch that one off and sit in his chair, letting the big chair engulf me. It's like it's holding me, like I'm safe.

The container of lube sits open on the desk. I take it, close it, put it back in the desk drawer. I go through each of them in turn, methodically, nonchalantly. I'm not afraid, for some reason. Maybe it's stupid. He just told me how he'd punish me the next time, but I'm not afraid.

Because Killian Black may be the answer to everything.

Because Killian Black can help me collect my pounds of flesh.

But I can't tell him why. I can't ever tell him what happened. We promised each other, Jones and I, that we would never tell.

Shame gurgles in my belly, threatening to paralyze me. I forego the empty tumbler and bring the bottle of whiskey to my mouth. The stuff burns, but it works faster than the wine. My head's already fuzzy. I force another long swallow, then set it down. Close my eyes against the shame. Squeeze the heels of my hands into them.

When I open them again, I see how my mascara smears them black. I don't care though. I open another drawer, the last one, and inside it, light catches the black metal of a pistol, making it shine bright. I look at it for a long minute. Reach down for it. Wrap my trembling hand over the butt of it.

The steel is cold to the touch. Solid in its weight. In its promise.

I set it on the desk and stare at it. Hate fills me, rage creeps along that hate. Years of it. Years of being powerless. I sit up straighter and a plan begins to take form in my head.

Killian Black is the answer.

There's no such thing as coincidence. Everything happens for a reason. This is why I'm here.

I glance up at the monitors. The one set to the restaurant shows Kill sitting at a table with Hugo and a man I don't recognize. The man is smaller than both of them. He has his head in his hands and is shaking it. Kill grips a handful of his hair and tugs it back. My curiosity grows and I watch, wishing I could hear but this camera doesn't have a speaker. At least not one that I can find. The man nods something and Kill releases him. Hugo takes him by the scruff of his neck and stands him up. Kill gets up too, but then a woman stops him. She puts her hands on his shoulders and Kill smiles at her. It's a smile I haven't seen, there's something almost tender about it.

I lean in to watch, looking closer, recognizing her as one of the strippers. Brandy, I think? She's the wannabe lawyer. Lawyer my ass.

He gestures for her to sit. She does and so does he, motioning to the waitress to bring them a drink. They talk for a minute, then the waitress brings them their drinks. Champagne for her. A bottle of it. An expensive one. Whiskey for him. He's still smiling while she talks. She's very animated and I hate her and her pretty blonde hair and her perfect stripper's body. And the more he laughs at what she's saying, the more relaxed he appears, the more I hate her.

I lean back, still watching, eyes narrowed on her. I reach

for the bottle of whiskey and take another swig. But when she leans in and takes one of his hands in both of hers, I'm done. I get up, pick up my purse. It's ridiculous I brought one. It's empty but for the tube of lipstick I was allowed. I don't even have my wallet, my driver's license. I have nothing. I am completely at his mercy. But if he thinks I'm going to sit here while he's down in the club flirting with a stripper after fucking me, he's got another thing coming.

At the elevator, I realize something. There's no button to push. There's a key pad. And I don't know the code.

"Fuck!"

I turn back around to his desk, switch off all the damn monitors because fuck him. I don't want this. He doesn't need me. He can fuck his stripper. His strippers. He doesn't need to keep me locked up.

I pick up the gun. I've never fired one before. I've never even held one. I take it in both hands like I've seen in movies and aim it straight ahead at the elevator. I imagine Judge Callahan's face there. I put my finger on the trigger.

Just when I do the doors slide open and Kill's surprised face comes into view.

"What the—"

I'm just as surprised as he is, but his reaction comes much more swiftly than mine. I swear it takes him all of a millisecond to lunge to the desk. To get behind me as I stumble. To catch me. Disarm me.

"What the hell are you doing?" he roars.

I'm on the floor and he's looming over me and it's like all that whiskey hits me at once.

He's checking the gun. Taking something out of it. I guess it was loaded.

"Cilla, what the fuck are you doing?" He sees the bottle of whiskey, turns back to me with a raised eyebrow.

I try to stand, but it's too hard, so I decide to lay down instead.

"I don't know why you want me here," I hear my words slur together. "I mean, you have Brandy. Brandy? Whiskey? Bourbon? What's her name again?"

"Did you drink all this?" he asks, pointing to the half empty bottle.

I blink up at him. He's a giant and from down here, he looks a hundred feet tall. "You don't scare me, you know." I roll onto my side. I need to sleep. I am so tired all of a sudden, it's like my eyelids are sticky with glue.

I hear a chuckle, feel his strong arms lift me, turn my face into him and smell his cologne. I force my eyes to open and point a finger into his chest.

"Do you fuck her?" I hear myself ask.

"What are you talking about?" He's still holding me and dialing a number on his cell phone at the same time.

"I saw you. Ordering champagne," I drag out the last word, try to roll my eyes but it hurts my head and they just close instead. "See, that's what I mean. I mean, you can fuck anyone. Why do you want me?"

"I need the car around back, John. I'll be down in a minute," he says into the phone. "And get Cilla's coat out of coat check."

He sets me down on the sofa and I look up at him. He's taking off his jacket, wrapping it over my shoulders. I can't even keep my head up and feel it loll into his chest when he lifts me up again.

"I'm sleepy."

"I bet you are."

We get into the elevator. I just keep my eyes closed as we ride down, my face buried in his chest. I keep it that way when I hear the music. We're on the main floor. But a few minutes later, a door opens and a sudden gust of wind makes me shiver.

Kill unloads me into the backseat of a sedan. He gets in beside me. "Penthouse."

"Yes, sir."

I open my eyes to find him watching me, shaking his head. "You don't listen."

"Why did you leave your shoes there?" I ask, that question suddenly the most important thing in the world.

"What?" He acts surprised, but I know he knows what. I see it on his face.

I sigh a deep breath in, then out, and when the car turns a corner, I slide into Kill's shoulder. He sighs too, lays my head on his lap, draws his jacket up over my arm.

"Sleep it off, sweetheart." I feel his hands on my hair, brushing it away from my face, and when it closes over my shoulder, I do just as he says. I sleep.

16

KILL

Cilla doesn't sleep peacefully. It's three in the morning and I'm watching her. She keeps throwing the covers off, muttering angry words, then quiet whispers. It's not those that make me keep vigil, though. It's when she curls up. When she tucks her face into her arms. When she begins to cry.

Every time I touch her, she jumps, and I think I've woken her but I haven't. She's too drunk to wake up. Trapped in whatever nightmare world the whiskey and the past have created for her. She only settles into a calm sleep when the sun begins to rise. And only after speaking the words that give me pause: "I'll take the pounds of flesh, Jones."

Pounds of flesh.

"What the hell happened to you, Cilla?" I ask, drawing her to me, wrapping an arm around her and listening to her breathe against my chest.

The next time I open my eyes is when Cilla stirs awake. I watch her roll onto her back. Mascara is smeared across her face and left its trace on the white pillowcase. She blinks, touches her forehead, groans and closes her eyes again, turning onto her side.

I smile. "Headache?"

Her eyes are wide when she shifts again, looking at me, looking around the room. Remembering.

"I feel like I'm going to die."

I get up, walk toward the bathroom. "You won't die, but you'll have less incentive to drink a half bottle of whisky after this morning." I open the medicine cabinet, get two aspirin and fill a cup with water before returning to the bedroom.

She looks me over. I'm wearing a pair of boxer briefs. She sits up, peeking beneath the blankets, drawing them up to cover herself.

"I took off your clothes."

"I see that."

"Don't worry, I didn't fuck you while you were passed out."

She blushes, eyes the pills. "What are they?"

"Aspirin."

She takes them, sets them on her tongue, takes two sips of water and gives me the glass back.

"Why on earth did you think it was a good idea to drink that much?"

She shakes her head, closes her eyes. I can see she's hurting. I take a deep breath in. "It might help if you eat something."

"I don't think I can keep anything down."

"Just lay back down then. Sleep a little longer."

She nods. "I have to pee."

I push the covers back and offer my hand. She grabs the edge of the comforter to try to cover herself and slides off the bed, almost falling until I catch her.

"I've seen you naked already, remember?" I walk her into the bathroom, lift the lid of the toilet and sit her down.

"Can you go away?"

"No."

"You like humiliating me?"

"In this case, I don't want you to fall over and crack your head open on my bathroom floor."

At that, she lowers her lashes, obviously agreeing it's a possibility but not wanting to give me the satisfaction of admitting it. A moment later, she pees. It's a quiet trickle. I wait for her to wipe, then help her stand and flush the toilet. She washes her hands, pushes the hair from her face as she looks at her reflection.

"I look like I feel."

"No, I'm guessing you feel a lot worse. Come on."

She lets me take her back to bed. Once she's in, I tuck the comforter up to her chin.

"Why did you have the gun pointing at me?"

She shrugs. "It's not what you think. I wasn't pointing at you. I didn't know you were coming up just then."

"Why did you pick it up at all? I mean, I understand you would go through my things even though I told you not to. It's your nature to be...difficult."

"I'm not—"

"Have you ever even handled a gun before?"

"No. I've never touched one. I just saw it and..." she trails off.

"What? And what?" I watch her and she me, and I know she's trying to decide if she's going to tell me or not. "You said some strange things last night, Cilla."

"I was drunk. Drunk people say strange things."

"No, not then. In your sleep. You said, and I quote, *'I'll take the pounds of flesh, Jones'*. What does that mean?"

She quickly shifts her gaze, her cheeks reddening. She knows exactly what I'm talking about.

"You said your brother's name. Several times."

"I have to sleep." She rolls onto her side, facing away from me.

"What happened? What do you have to free yourselves from?"

She burrows deeper into the comforter. I wait for her answer, and it takes her a long time to talk. I think I hear her sniffle, but I don't push it.

"Thank you for taking care of me. You didn't have to do that, I guess."

She's not going to tell me. Not now.

"You took care of me the other night." I mean when I walked in after my middle of the night trip to the barn. I mean when she wouldn't leave me alone when I told her to. Because the last thing I wanted that night was to be alone.

I walk out of the bedroom and close the door behind me.

IT'S LATE AFTERNOON WHEN I HEAR THE COFFEE MACHINE GO on. I get up from my desk, walk out of the study to find Cilla in the kitchen. She has the makings of a sandwich on the counter and is nibbling on a piece of bread. Her hair's wet from a shower and she's wrapped in a bathrobe. I remember she doesn't actually have any clothes here.

"I'll send someone out to pick up some clothes."

"I have a closet full of clothes in my apartment. It's only about twenty minutes from her."

"That's fine." I approach the counter.

She looks at me, confused. "Does that mean I can go there?"

"It means I'll send someone."

"What do you think I'm going to do? Run? Call for help?"

"I just like to keep you close."

"Why?"

"Because."

"Do you fuck the strippers?"

I'm taken aback. "What?"

"The girl from last night. I watched you with her. Saw how you looked at her—"

"How did I look at her?"

She turns her stubborn chin up, sucks in her cheeks. "I saw you order a bottle of champagne," she says before busying herself with making her sandwich.

I walk around the counter, take her arms, make her face me. "Are you jealous?"

She gives me an incredulous look. Like nothing could be further from the truth. But the flush of her cheeks gives her away and I grin.

"You're jealous."

"No, of course I'm not."

"Yes, you are."

She straightens and looks at me, suddenly angry, probably because I'm onto her. "I just think you should be using condoms with me if you're going to fuck your strippers."

I laugh outright, release her and take the slice of cheese off her bread. I stick it in my mouth. "I'm not fucking anyone else."

"I saw how—"

"I'm not fucking anyone else, Cilla. Don't be jealous, it's not becoming." I open the fridge, grab the juice.

"What does that even mean?"

I turn to face her, find her standing with her hands on her hips.

"Which part?" I take the lid off the carton and drink straight from it.

"You know what? Piss off." She turns her back on me, puts another slice of bread on her sandwich and picks it up like she's going to walk way.

I grab her arm and spin her around.

"You don't get to tell me to piss off. And you don't get to walk away."

"Let me go."

I don't. "I told you I'm not fucking anyone else."

"I don't care if you are."

I take the sandwich from her hand and bite into it, then set it on the counter and release her. When she makes to scoot away, I trap her with a hand on either side.

"I think you do care," I say in a low voice.

She stares up at me, not denying it. "I want something from you," she says instead.

This is a turn I didn't expect. "What do you want?"

"Two things, actually."

My eyebrows go up.

"I want to see Jones."

I expect this one but I have a feeling it's the second thing that's going to throw me. "And?"

She searches my eyes, caution in hers, the battle of whether or not to trust me.

"And I want you to help me get my pound of flesh."

17

CILLA

Kill's watching me closely, yet his eyes betray nothing. I want to know what he's thinking. What he knows about me.

"You're dark, Cilla." His eyes move to my mouth. Down to the exposed skin of my chest. With one hand, he undoes the belt holding the robe together so it falls open. He looks down at me, at the space between my breasts, at the slit of my sex. His eyes glide back up to mine. "Whose flesh?"

"Herbert Callahan."

"*Judge* Herbert Callahan."

"How do you know?"

"I know. Why? What did he do to you?" he lifts me up, sits me on the counter, pushes my legs wide. Even when he just looks at me like that, with that wild hunger in his eyes, he makes me wet.

"I can't tell you that."

"You want me to kill a judge but you can't tell me why?"

"I never asked you to kill him. I said I wanted your help, that's all. I want to feel his blood on my hands."

He studies me for an eternity. I reach out to touch the scar on his face. I trace it.

"Did it hurt?"

"I don't remember."

I move my hand to his lips. His chin. Down to his chest. Over his powerful arms. He's wearing a T-shirt today. I pull it out of his jeans, push it up until he slides it over his head and tosses it aside.

"You have secrets," he says, pushing me backward, opening my robe wide and dipping his head between my legs. "And I want them. That's why I want you."

I touch his head, pull it into me, arch my back when he takes my clit into his mouth.

"You want to own everything," I say, wrapping my legs around his neck. "You want me inside and out. You can't, though. Not this time."

He raises his head, meets my eyes. "I always get what I want."

I push him back between my legs. I want his mouth on me. "Will you help me?"

He dips his tongue inside me before returning to my clit, teasing it, then sucking hard, making me cry out. Making me squeeze my legs tight around his neck as he slides one hand up to my breast, pinches my nipple.

"Fuck," I mutter, closing my eyes. His tongue is soft, the scruff of his jaw rough, and I come. I come on his tongue as we negotiate murder. I come hard as he tells me he'll possess me. Own every part of me.

I'm gasping for breath when I loosen my legs from his neck. He straightens, looks down at me, doesn't wipe his glistening lips. Instead, with one hand, he undoes his jeans, pushes them down. He leans over me, thrusting into me so hard, my breath catches. He brings his face to mine, kisses me. I taste myself on his lips, his tongue, and I open for him. He's rough, fucking me hard, and it's not long before I'm coming again, clinging to him, digging my nails into his shoulders as he mutters a curse, his mouth still against mine, his breath short gasps as I feel him come inside me, filling me up.

When he pulls out of me, he lays a hand on my belly, holding me down. He's watching cum spill out of me, I feel its warmth slide down my thighs. He looks at me as I rise to a seat, snakes his hand up my back, to my neck and into my hair and kisses me roughly, drawing me to stand. When he's done kissing me, he keeps his hand at the back of my head, holds me close, his eyes unreadable.

"Tell me why."

I shake my head no.

He squeezes his fingers in my hair, making me flinch.

"What did he do to you?" he asks.

I can't tell him. I promised Jones. Besides, if I did, he'd be repulsed by me and some part of me, it needs him. It needs Killian Black. Needs him to want me.

"Will you help me?"

He releases me, steps back, tucks his dick into his briefs and pulls his jeans closed. All the while, he doesn't release me from his gaze.

"You don't want blood on your hands, Cilla."

That's not what I expect. Not what I want to hear. "I know what I want."

He shakes his head. "Tell me why."

"I told you I can't. Can't you help me without asking that one thing? Can't you leave that one piece of me to me?"

"I'll kill him for you, I'll make it slow. Pound by pound if that's what you want. But you need to tell me why."

"I don't want you to kill him for me. *I* want to take the pound of flesh. *Me*."

He shakes his head. "It's not poetry, that." He touches my cheek. "You're not cut out—"

"You don't know me!" I yell. Kill stands watching. If he's shocked or even surprised, he doesn't show it. This man is like a vault, everything locked up tight, yet he wants everything from me. Wants me stripped naked. Laid bare.

I fist my hands at my sides, punch them into his chest. He takes my wrists, holds me there.

"You don't know anything about me, Killian Black!" I hear how my voice has changed, hear it break. I try to pull free, but I can't. "I thought you would help me."

"I will. I already told you I will. I just need to know why."

I shake my head and this time, when I try to break free, he releases me. I run into the bedroom. His. It's where we slept last night. But I stop, shake my head, back up into the hallway. He's standing at the other end of it watching me, so I turn, and I run into another room. The one he'd put me in the first night. I slam the door shut and slap my hands onto my face, press against my eyes.

"Cilla."

"Leave me alone," I manage. I'm not screaming anymore.

He opens the door, but I can't look at him. I run into the bathroom and close the door, sit with my back to it and I cry. I just sit there and weep. There's no sound, and somehow, I'm calm but I can't stop crying. I can't stop the tears and there's just so many of them, a never-ending waterfall. And even when I know he's gone, I just keep sitting there, weeping.

I was close. So close. But it's gone now. All my strength of the night before, it's gone. That sliver of light, of hope, it's being washed away by this unending fall of tears.

18

KILL

The one thing I don't need right now is fucking Benji in the lobby. Cilla's in her room falling apart. I'm standing here like some asshole not knowing what the fuck to do for the first time in my life, and my idiot cousin chooses this moment to show up.

"Send him up," I growl into the phone.

I text Hugo in the meantime. He checked in early this morning to tell me he'd landed but I haven't heard from him since.

"Anything yet?" I text.

"Nothing. I'm about to knock on an old housekeeper's door."

Of course he'd have nothing. Callahan is no fool. He won't leave a trail.

"Keep me posted."

"She's about ninety-four so I don't expect much."

"Let me know anyway."

The elevator doors slide open and Benji steps off wearing a big grin and those stupid shoes with the platforms again. His eyes bounce around the room and he's holding his hands together nervously like an addict in withdrawal.

"Ben," I say. "What are you doing here?"

"I didn't like how we left things."

I just look at him.

"Can I have a drink?" he asks.

"It's early for that, isn't it?"

He's agitated, on edge. "I just need a drink."

"Sit down." I pour him a whiskey and sit across from him. "What are you doing here, Ben?"

He swallows half the whiskey before speaking. "I want you to know I'm loyal to you. We're family."

I sit and silently wait.

"What my father did, it was wrong. Didn't feel right I brought that up the other night. Ginny was a good friend to me."

I nod my head. He's the last person I want to talk about this with, but he's right. He and Ginny were friends and her death impacted him badly. It's one of the reasons I've always felt a responsibility to him.

"You came here to tell me that?"

"No, there's something else. I need your help."

Ah. "What now?"

"I'm in trouble, Kill. Real trouble."

"What was it, two months since you were last in real trouble?"

"It's worse this time. For real."

"M-hm."

"I owe money."

"Same trouble, different day."

He sighs. Grits his teeth.

"Is that why you put Jones up to stealing that bag of coke from me?"

"I wasn't stealing from you. It's Benedetti's coke."

"You know I almost broke both his arms and legs for it, right? Yet you walk away scot-free."

"But you didn't," Ben says, surprising me with his seemingly sudden sobriety. His rage. His knowledge.

"Watch your tone."

He takes a deep breath, drinks more of the whiskey.

"How much do you owe?"

"Twenty-grand."

"Hefty sum," I say, eyebrows raised.

He drinks some more.

"To whom do you owe twenty-thousand-dollars?"

Here he hesitates and I have a feeling I'm not going to like his answer.

"Who, Ben?"

"Arturo Antonino."

He has the grace to hang his head. I stand up, shaking my head as I look at the top of his. "I can't help you this time, cousin, but I think you already knew that."

"What?"

"You heard me."

"Why not?"

I go to him, push my finger into his forehead, poke him while I speak to make my point. "Because he's Benedetti's enemy which means he's my enemy. I'm not putting twenty-grand into his pocket. I'm not fucking stupid."

"You don't understand, he'll fucking kill me!"

"He won't kill you but he will beat you and maybe you'll learn something." I check my watch. "What the fuck are you doing borrowing from him anyway?"

"I didn't borrow it. I was at a poker game—"

"Why am I not surprised?" I check my watch. I want him gone. "I have a meeting in a few minutes, Ben."

I hear the shower go on just then. Cilla. Ben glances down the hall, then looks at me, eyebrows raised.

"Your meeting having a shower?"

I don't want him to know about Cilla. "Yeah. She is. And she'll get anxious if I don't get in there."

"Girl from last night? Jones's sister, right?"

How the fuck does he know? "Time to go, Ben." I push the button to open the elevator doors. He glances down the hall again, looks like he wants to say something, but shakes his head and steps onto the elevator.

"Enjoy your meeting," he says, handing me the empty cup and putting the word meeting in air quotes.

I don't respond, but watch him until the elevator doors close. This conversation isn't over, I know, but right now I have another priority. I walk to the guest room where the shower has switched off. I knock before entering. Cilla's there in the same bathrobe combing her fingers through her hair.

"What do you want?" She folds her arms across her chest.

"You ready to go pick up some clothes?"

She watches me. "From my apartment?"

I nod.

She nods too, like she's scared to talk and fuck it up.

"I'll take you to see Jones after that."

"Why?"

"Because you asked me."

"So you suddenly decide to be nice to me?"

"I guess so."

"I asked you for something else too."

"And I asked you to tell me why. I can't agree until I know the whole story." I take a step toward her. "I'll find out anyway, Cilla. I've got a man in Florida who's about to meet with the judge." Slight exaggeration, but close enough to truth.

"You what?" Panic widens her jade eyes.

"It might be best if you tell me yourself," I say.

The way she looks at me, it's like she's trying to figure out if I'm bluffing. "Just leave it alone," she says, clearly deciding to take her chances. "Please."

"No."

Cilla's apartment is in a building about thirty minutes from mine. It's in a decent neighborhood. Not one I'd live in, but not bad. I follow her up the stairs to the second floor. When we reach her door, she stops and turns to me.

"I don't have my key."

I take it out of my pocket and hand it to her.

She rolls her eyes. "Of course." She slides it into the lock and turns it. "Do you have my wallet too? My driver's license? Credit cards?"

"And the twenty-four dollars you had on you."

She rolls her eyes, shakes her head, pushes the door open, walks inside. I follow her in.

"Everything is safe. You'll get it all back in one month."

"You mean when I've done my time?" she mutters as she walks through the living room, switching on lights as she goes.

I look around the place. It's not big. In fact, her entire apartment can just about fit into the living room/kitchen of the penthouse. But it's neat, not much out of place. The kitchen counter is spotless, appliances not brand new, but not old either, and clean. I open her fridge. Inside is a container of what I am guessing is expired milk, various jars of jam, and an open bottle of wine that's not quite half-full. I walk around the counter that divides the kitchen from the living room where a sweater hangs over the back of the couch. Her laptop is on the small dining room table. Papers are stacked neatly beside it.

When she emerges a few moments later, she's wearing a pair of sweats, an oversized hoodie and Chucks.

"Don't approve?" she asks me, cocking her head to the side.

"That depends." I make a sign for her to spin around.

She holds her middle finger up at me and I have to chuckle. "Careful, Cilla. My palm's feeling twitchy."

She gives me a glare, then moves toward her computer, packs the folders and the laptop into the tote bag beside the chair and looks up at me. "Okay, ready."

"I gave you a computer."

"And as much as I appreciate the upgrade, there's nothing wrong with this one. I haven't even turned the new one on. Maybe you can return it. Get your money back."

"Fine. Let's go."

She seems surprised, which is what I want. I open the door and gesture for her to go ahead. She does and once we're in the hallway, I lock the door and pocket the key. We take the stairs back down to my SUV.

"Where is Jones?" she asks once we get on the road.

"At a facility about forty-five minutes from here."

"Facility?"

"Your brother has a drug problem, Cilla." She doesn't deny it, but she's also not confronting the fact. "You can't not know this."

"He was clean." She looks out the side window. "He tried to stay clean. I told him he shouldn't be around it. Get a decent job somewhere. Pack groceries if he has to." She turns to me again. "I told him he could move in with me. At least until he could be on his own without having to work for..." She steels herself. "For men like you."

"Men like me?"

She just looks up at me, and I know she's scared but she's also being honest. And she's right. But I'm also the guy footing the bill for the detox center.

"No, he probably shouldn't work for men like me."

"So you put him in a detox center?"

"Yes."

"Why?"

"I needed to keep an eye on him anyway, in case you bailed on our deal. This is cheaper than having men on him 24/7."

"I can't imagine it's cheaper."

It's not, but I don't react.

"Is he doing okay?" she asks a moment later.

"He's detoxing."

She nods.

"Kill?"

I glance at her, curious at how she's looking at me. "Yes?"

"Don't mention Callahan to him, okay?"

"Curiouser and curiouser."

"Just don't. Please."

I nod, but don't state the fact that I already have. She'll find out soon enough. I pull into the parking lot of Dover Recovery Village and park the car. The facility is an old mansion that was converted into what it is today thirty years ago. It's small and it's expensive, but it's the best.

Cilla looks from the building to me, eyebrows raised.

I get out of the car. "Let's go."

She meets me at the front of the car and we walk up the half-dozen steps to the front doors. I open one and she enters, then follows me to the nurse sitting behind the large desk.

The nurse does a double take, then stands. "Mr. Black."

I nod. "We're here to see Jones Hawking."

"We didn't know you'd be coming again so soon."

"Again?" Cilla asks me.

I ignore her. "This is Priscilla Hawking. Jones's sister."

"Nice to meet you, Ms. Hawking."

"How's my brother."

"He's doing well, considering. I don't think Doctor Moore is here, but let me double check and otherwise, I'll walk you up."

"Who's Dr. Moore?" Cilla asks.

"He's your brother's primary physician," the nurse says and walks away.

Cilla turns to me. "What did she mean when she said she didn't know you'd be coming again so soon?"

"I paid Jones a visit yesterday."

"What?"

"I'm responsible for his care. I want to be sure I'm getting my money's worth, that's all."

"That's all?"

"That's all."

"I don't believe you."

"I don't care."

The nurse clears her throat. "Ready?" she asks when we look at her.

"Yes," Cilla says.

We follow the nurse to the stairs where a man is painting the banister. The carpet needs replacing—I guess there's much more foot traffic these days than the house originally had. We head up to the second floor and walk quietly down the hall. Jones is in the last room. I watch Cilla as she takes in the various sounds and smells of the place. It's obvious she's never been somewhere like this.

"This is it." The nurse stops. There's an orderly stationed outside his door.

"Why is he here?" she asks.

The nurse glances at me. "Your brother's been...upset."

Cilla follows the nurse's gaze to me. "Upset how?"

"Let's go in," I say.

Cilla faces me, puts her hands on my chest. "No. I'll go in alone."

"If he gets violent—"

"He's had a mild sedative," the nurse points out, clearly uncomfortable.

Cilla spins around. "Why?"

The nurse clears her throat, looks at me. She obviously knows who I am and she's inclined not to upset me.

"Just go in, Cilla." I check my watch. "You have fifteen minutes."

"Fifteen minutes?"

I raise an eyebrow. "Fourteen minutes and forty-five seconds."

She lets out an exasperated breath, then nods to the nurse. The orderly opens the door. Jones is lying on the bed, his skin flushed, sickly looking. He looks a little worse than he did when I last saw him.

"Cilla," he says, sitting up, his movements slow.

"Jones!" she runs to him, leans down. I expect her to hug him but she stops short.

Jones looks over her shoulder, finds me standing there. His eyes widen. Cilla must feel the shift because she straightens, turns to me.

"You said I had fifteen minutes. Alone."

"Thirteen," I say, then walk out into the hallway. "Door stays open."

The nurse looks at me. The orderly stands there like he doesn't see how awkward this all is.

"Thank you, nurse. I'll take it from here."

"Yes, sir."

I take my phone out and scroll through emails while standing close enough to hear, but their voices are whispers, and I can't make out what either of them are saying. There's a moment where Jones becomes animated, but Cilla manages to quiet him. When the time is up, I step into the room and clear my throat.

"Time, Cilla."

"Just one more minute." Her back is to me. She's sitting on the edge of the bed but I notice they're not really touching. His eyes jump from me to her and he leans in to whisper something.

"It's okay. I'll take care of everything," she replies to whatever he says. She stands. "I'll come back to see you next week." She gives me a pointed look, but I don't care about any promises she makes him. We'll see next week. "I love you," she says, and it sounds awkward.

Jones nods, looks at his lap. The few times I've seen Jones, he was animated, probably high or stoned. Now, he just looks pathetic.

A few minutes later, we're out in the parking lot. Cilla turns to me when we get to the SUV.

"You scared him. He's detoxing and you scared the shit out of him."

"I wanted answers and since I'm the one paying for this, I think I have some right to ask."

"You have no right. We never asked for this. Neither of us

asked you to do this. The deal was me. Me for one month. It didn't come with strings!"

"That deal changed the minute you asked for my help collecting your pound of flesh. We've got all kinds of strings now."

She shakes her head. "No. That has nothing to do with you. I don't agree to your terms. I take back what I said. What I asked for."

"That's not how things work."

"It is in my world and you're in my world now, aren't you, sweetheart?"

She exhales.

My attention shifts to the side door where two nurses walk out at the end of their shift. "Get in. We'll talk at the house."

"No. I don't want to talk about this with you. This isn't part of our deal, period."

I take her arm, walk her around to the passenger side. "We're not having this discussion until you cool down."

"Until I cool down?" She digs her feet into the ground just as I open her door. "No. You have my body for thirty days. You can't have the rest of me."

I look down at her, see the panic in her eyes, the desperation. "Get in, Cilla. No one needs to know our business."

She looks over my shoulder at the nurses who've now stopped and are openly watching us. "Killian, please. I'm asking you to please leave this be."

"I'm low on patience here. Get in."

It takes her another minute but she exhales and climbs into the SUV. I reach across her to buckle her belt. She lets me. When I close the door, my cell phone rings. I pull it out of my pocket and swipe the button to accept the call.

"About time," I say.

"No one's talking," Hugo answers.

"What do you mean? Make them talk. Isn't that your specialty?"

"The old woman either couldn't or wouldn't say anything. Had to talk through her daughter. But when I showed her photos of Jones and the girl, her face went white."

I glance at Cilla who's watching me through the window.

"Why didn't you push her?"

"She's in her nineties. I didn't want her to drop dead on my account. Besides, her daughter wanted me out when she saw how upset her mother got. She threatened to call the cops." He takes a breath. "I did hear the old woman say one thing before I walked out though. One word. Devil."

"Go back. I don't care what it takes. I want to know what happened in that house."

I hang up the phone. Walk around to the driver's side of the car and climb in. I start the car but before putting it in drive, I turn to her.

"I just want to know one thing. That's all," I say.

She sits watching me for a long while before she speaks. "What?"

"Did Callahan touch you?" As I say it, I feel rage build inside me. It fucking burns. She would have been Ginny's age. If that old man laid a fucking finger on her—

But her answer breaks into that thought.

"No."

One word. She doesn't even blink.

And I don't believe her.

"If he did, I'll help you get your pound of flesh. I just want to hear it from you."

"He didn't rape me." She doesn't struggle to say the word I couldn't.

It's me who takes time to react now and eventually, I nod, although I don't know why, and put the car in drive. We don't talk for the entire ride back to Rockcliffe House and once we're there, she turns to me.

"My headache is back. Do you mind if I go to bed?" She's asking permission. It's unlike her.

"That's fine."

I watch her climb the stairs, note how she looks a little more tired.

"Cilla," I call out.

She stops when she's almost reached the top, but she doesn't turn to me.

"I'm going to find out."

Without a word, she walks up the remaining stairs and disappears into her room.

19

CILLA

The sun is just breaking the horizon when I wake. I feel like I can't breathe, like there's a rope getting tighter and tighter around my neck. It seems like the past has swept right into the present, and like a tidal wave, it's about to wash everything away.

Me with it.

Jones wasn't good. Kill had asked him about Callahan and considering the state he was in, I feel like it set him back eight years. That's how it's always been with Jones. He's too broken to ever be fixed. I know that. I've known it a long time.

Kill asking me that question in the car, he had no right. It's not his to know. Why can't he accept that I can't tell him?

I should never have asked him for help. That was a mistake. Because I fully believe he will find out. And what will happen then?

Shame begins to spread its dark shadow through me. I force a deep breath in, then out. I look up to the canopy over my borrowed bed, remembering how he'd filmed me. How he could be watching me now. I push the covers off and stand on the bed, but the canopy is too high to reach. I climb down, go into the closet to look for something I can use to bring it down. To break the camera he uses to spy on me. I find nothing.

Back in the bedroom, I look around until my gaze falls on the lamp on the nightstand. I remove the shade and pick up the long, thin body. The base makes it heavier than I expect, but I unplug it and climb back up on the bed to start poking at the folded cloth. Dust makes me sneeze and squint my eyes but eventually, metal clangs on metal and I locate it. Drawing my arm back, I swing hard. It takes two times but soon, pieces of the camera are lying on the bed. I stumble off, still not satisfied until I smash it to bits, until I'm out of breath.

I stand back and drop the lamp, wipe off my hands, then walk into the bathroom, have a shower, get dressed and pull my hair into a ponytail, pinning the flyaway strands back. I don't bother to conceal the evidence of what I've done. I don't care.

It's still early when I step into the hallway. I glance down the hall at his room, wonder if he's there. At the bottom of the stairs, I look at his study door. There's no one around so I go to it, wiggle the handle. He's more than peeking into my life so why not? Why shouldn't I peek into his? But it's locked.

As I near the kitchen, I smell coffee and hear talking. I push the swinging door open to find Helen and one of the girls who'd served us dinner the first night preparing some food.

"Good morning," I say.

"Good morning. You're up early."

I give her a broad, unnatural smile, feeling almost manic. I then walk to the coffee machine, pick up a cup and push some buttons. Helen comes over and takes the cup from my hand to push the right button.

"Thank you," I say. When the coffee's ready, I take my mug. "Is that bacon?" I ask, smelling it as the girl lays slices into a pan.

"Yes, shall I make you some?"

"Yes, please. And scrambled eggs. I'm starving this morning."

"Right away. Go and have a seat and I'll bring—"

"I'll wait here. Thanks." I sip my coffee.

Helen looks at me like she's surprised, then resumes her work. "Suit yourself."

"Is Kill here?"

"No, he left last night."

"Did he say when he'd be back?"

"No, dear."

Perfect. I sip my coffee while the girl scrambles two eggs next to the frying bacon. When it's ready, I take the plate from the tray Helen is preparing.

"I'll eat in the library." I turn to leave. "Oh, and Helen, my room needs to be cleaned up. I made a bit of a mess, I'm afraid." I want her kept busy because I have a plan.

"I'll go up there in about fifteen minutes."

"Thank you." I walk out of the kitchen and to the library where I eat my breakfast with the door open, and, like clockwork, I hear Helen climb the stairs exactly fifteen minutes later.

Leaving my empty dish in the library, I pull two pins out of my hair and head to Kill's study.

One thing living in Judge Callahan's house taught me

and my brother was how to pick a lock. It was the only way we'd get to see each other some days.

I'm bending one of the hair pins as I glance around to make sure no one is near, although at this point I almost don't care. I take hold of the doorknob, squat down so I'm at eye level and stick the bent hairpin into it. Keeping pressure on this one, I begin to test the pins with the other. I'm out of practice, but this shouldn't be too hard. When I was here the other night, I saw it was a simple lock.

The vacuum cleaner goes on upstairs as I work my way through the pins and, not ten minutes later, the final one clicks and I can turn the doorknob. Exhaling a sigh of relief, I straighten and push the door open, just as I hear another door open behind me.

A chill runs up my spine and I don't have to turn around to know it's him. I feel him, like I do whenever he enters a room. He uses up too much space, hogs too much oxygen.

He takes two steps. Stops. Closes the door. I hear his keys jangle as he puts them in his pocket.

The vacuum cleaner switches off and Kill moves, footsteps approaching me. He doesn't speak, not at first. Instead, he comes up close behind me, closes his hand over mine which is still on the doorknob. Leans his body against mine, breathes against my neck before walking me into his study, plastering my back against the door as he pushes it closed. He takes my wrists, draws my arms over my head, his eyes dark as they roam over my face.

I swallow. It's that look in his eyes, the wild one. The one that makes me want.

"What are you looking for, sweetheart?"

"I busted your camera, you freak."

His eyes roam my face. He grins. "Did you, now?" He presses against me. He's hard.

I lick my lips. "Yes."

He dips his head down, kisses my mouth and, eyes open, I kiss him back. When he draws away, I look him over. He's still wearing what he had on yesterday.

"Where were you?"

"Thinking," he says, kissing me again. His hands are undoing the buttons of my jeans, but he doesn't push them off. Instead, once he's unzipped them, he slides his hand inside and cups my sex.

I gasp.

"You're always wet for me."

"No."

He draws his hand out, smears his wet fingers across my cheek, my lip. He chuckles.

"Don't you want to know what I've been thinking?" he asks.

He wraps the hand that was just inside my panties through my hair, tugs my head backward so my mouth opens.

"Don't you want to know?" he prods.

"No."

He kisses my chin. My throat. That hollow above my collarbone. He straightens, his face suddenly harder. Too hard. I scratch at his forearm, wanting to drag him off, but he's too strong so when I can't turn my head, I squeeze my eyes shut.

"Look at me, Cilla."

I shake my head as much as I can.

"You're no coward. Look at me."

I open my eyes, grit my teeth.

"I've been thinking I understand you."

I swallow hard, suddenly panicked at his words.

"See, I recognize something inside you. I know it. I get it.

You're brave and you're loyal, but you're also stubborn as fuck. I scare the shit out of you yet you constantly stand up to me. I told you once I liked taking but thing is, I think you like it when I make you. You need me to make you."

"Stop." I try to squirm away.

"It's the only way you can accept this. The only way you can come."

"Is that how you justify keeping me prisoner?"

He pushes my jeans down, cups my sex again, and he's right. I'm wet. Wet for him. I feel it. Hear it as he slips his fingers between my folds. He kisses my mouth, my cheek, brings his mouth to my ear.

"I know what you did before," he whispers.

He's playing with my clit and what I want to do is wrap my legs around his hips. I want him inside me. His fingers aren't enough. But I can't do that. I won't.

"Stop," I try. It's weak though. We both know it.

"No." He spins me around so one side of my face is pressed to the door. I hear him unzip his jeans and a moment later, he's inside me. My eyes close in relief as I feel myself stretch to take him. He groans and when he moves, he smashes my pelvic bone against the door.

"You like this," he says.

"Harder."

He grips a handful of hair, lifts me up, walks me to his desk. He shoves the papers off, swiping everything to the floor as he bends me over it, as he bends over me, his cock moving inside me, his breath at my ear.

"I know about The Black Swan."

I shudder like the room is freezing but it's not. He can't know about that. Can't know it's where I go when I need to take back control. When I start to feel things slipping away. I arch my back. "Harder." I squeeze my eyes shut, try to turn my face so I can't hear him, but he won't let me. The sound of our fucking is wet, and his breath is shallow. Sweat drops from his forehead onto my closed eyelid, slides over the bridge of my nose.

"I know, Cilla. I know."

I'm going to come soon. "You know that I fuck strangers? Good for you."

He draws back a little, slides his hand over my belly, down to my clit. I let out a moan when he pinches it.

"Open your eyes. Look at me."

I do, craning my neck a little. I see him at a strange angle, from the corner of one eye.

"It's about control with you. You never let them have it. But with me, you give it up."

"You take it. You make me."

"You *need* me to make you."

I don't speak. What is there to say?

"Did you even come with them?"

"Fuck you."

"No, I'm fucking you, sweetheart. Answer me."

I'm too close and I want to let go, but I'm fighting it too. Fighting him.

"Answer me, Cilla. Did you come with them like you do with me?"

I shake my head, close my eyes.

"I didn't think so." He pulls out, thrusts in so hard, I cry out, but it feels good. This feels so fucking good. "More?"

I nod.

"Say it."

I groan. I want this. I want it so badly.

"Beg for it, Cilla."

I'm so close, and he pulls out a little, teasing me with shallow thrusts when I hesitate.

"I hate you."

"Beg me."

"Please." I grunt with one of his thrusts. "Fuck me. Do it hard." I'm gripping the edges of the desk, a supplicant. "Please."

"Good girl," it's a low, deep growl and I hear the victory in his voice, but at least he stops talking. He's fucking me harder, deeper, like he's determined to touch the very core of me, and maybe he does. Maybe I let him. Maybe it's okay for him to know. For someone to know.

We come at the same time. His groan is muffled in my neck and when I cry out, he closes his hand over my mouth and we're both breathing hard and fast and when it's over, when he's filled me, we slide to the floor together and he holds me between his knees, our jeans half on, half off. I let my head fall into his chest. Let him hold me. We're both sweating and panting but we don't talk, not for a long time.

"I know it wasn't you he touched." His chin is on the top of my head and the moment his words register, my heart begins to pound. "I know it wasn't you he raped."

Slowly, so slowly, I turn my gaze up to meet his. His midnight eyes hold mine, steady, strong, in control.

"I know it was your brother. Is that why you did this? Why you take care of him? Guilt?"

I exhale. Relief softens the tension in my belly. He doesn't know. I almost want to laugh. It's sick, this is where I'm sick.

"I know he hurt you to force your brother to cooperate."

The memory is so vivid, I can almost feel the physical pain of the hammer. Almost hear the sound of my scream.

Of Jones's never-ending screams.

A tear slides down my face and I look away, unable to

stand the pity in his eyes. I'm not weak. This didn't break me. I refuse to let the fucking memory of it break me now.

Kill swipes his thumb across my cheek, wiping away the tear. "You're not responsible, Cilla. What that pervert did, it's on him. And if you want that pound of flesh, I'll get it for you."

20

KILL

What Hugo learned is fucked up.

I assumed Judge Callahan had raped Cilla. I didn't even consider any alternative. The way she was with her brother, so protective to the point she'd sacrifice herself, well, I just assumed he shared her secret. Kept it for her.

But I was wrong.

Hugo found the woman who'd gone public about the judge after her brother had committed suicide. They were foster kids he'd taken in before they'd taken Cilla and Jones in. She told Hugo her story, told him how she'd been shut down by the police and the media, being called a whore, a vengeful, ungrateful gold digger. She also told him how the judge wasn't ever interested in her. It was her brother he wanted. And the way he'd get the boy to cooperate was by hurting the girl. Making her scream in pain when he brought the hammer down on her hand while the brother watched, powerless.

And in turn, he made her watch when he raped her brother.

Jesus. I've seen some sick shit in my life, but this is the sickest.

I shake my head as I switch off the shower, wrap a towel around my hips and walk out of the bathroom. Cilla's sitting on the bed watching the bathroom door. Her wet hair hangs down her back and she's wearing different clothes but is barefoot.

"Come in," I say sarcastically.

"How will we do it?" she asks.

I study her. There's a strange look in her eyes. Something almost unhinged about her. Something wild. It only confirms my thinking that I need to do this myself.

"I'll take care of it."

She rises to her feet, shakes her head. "I don't want you to take care of it. I told you I want to do it."

"I know what you told me."

"Then why are you saying you'll take care of it?"

"Because frankly, I don't think you should be involved. You don't understand—"

"I understand what he did. What he took from us. Look at Jones. Just look at him. He's a goddamned mess."

"And you killing Callahan will change that how?"

She stops. Exhales loudly.

"Think about it. What will having this on your conscience do to you? Even knowing he's dead, it may not mean as much as you think or hope. I know people, Cilla. I know you. You're not a killer."

"You don't know me." She turns like she's going to walk away but I catch her arm, spin her to face me, take hold of both arms.

"Cilla, think." I give her a shake. "You need time to understand what this will mean for you. I know you'll come to your senses when you do."

"Come to my senses? What do you think? This will make you a good guy? Slay the dragon and be my fucking hero?"

I look down at her, but don't speak. She's not done yet, I see it in the way her fiercely beautiful, furious eyes shine.

"Callahan is *my* dragon. You have no right to take this away from me. I'm owed this."

"Have you thought about what happens if something doesn't go right? This is a judge we're talking about. And besides that, something like this, it damages you, Cilla. Permanently."

"I'm already damaged. Dark. You said so yourself."

"This is different. Just trust me, I know what I'm talking about."

She shoves me. "Go to hell." She walks away.

My hands fist at my sides, but I don't follow her.

"One thing before you go." She stops at the door, her back to me. "There's a party Saturday night at the club. I expect you to be there."

"I don't much feel like a party."

"Our deal still stands, whether you feel like it or not."

She turns. "When are you doing it?"

"I'm heading to Florida this afternoon."

"This isn't what I want. Not this way."

"It's better this way. You'll see."

"I won't." She pulls the door open and steps out into the hallway.

"And Cilla."

She stops.

"I'm no hero, not yours. Not anyone's. I've never aspired to be one."

21

CILLA

Kill is gone for the next three days. The one good thing to come out of this is that he arranges for someone to drive me to see Jones whenever I want while he's away. I'm also able to stay as long as I like. I guess this is his peace offering, but I don't accept it.

Watching my brother like this is hard, and knowing what's going to happen to Callahan doesn't make it easier. I thought it would. It's weird between Jones and me. It has been ever since the first time Callahan did what he did. The secret we keep, it's something that when I think about it, it makes me sick. It's disgusting. Wrong. What Kill said about it not being my fault, I know that, but thing is, it doesn't matter. It happened. It can't be undone.

Strange enough, it's worse now that I know what's going to happen. Now that Kill knows. Or thinks he knows. I guess over the last years, that shame has numbed. Never gone but suppressed. Never weakened, just kept at arm's length.

Jones isn't getting better. Maybe it's the detox itself. All the crap poisoning him as it leaves his system. But I'm not sure. He seems older now. Sadder.

We're sitting at the bay window of his room looking out at the mist over the vast gardens. It's early, but I wanted to be here early. He's wearing pajamas. I'm not sure if he's allowed to change out of them and chooses to keep them on or what, but I don't ask. We don't hold hands. We don't touch. We never touch.

"Do you think it'll ever go away?" he asks finally. He's not looking at me.

I've been waiting for this. I've known it's coming. We've been silent for eight years and this thing still owns us.

The skin around my eyes is wet but I don't move to wipe the tears away.

"He's going to kill him," I say, concentrating on the passing traffic on the road just beyond the property line.

Jones shifts his gaze to me. I meet it. His eyes are red and puffy like he's been crying for years. I guess in a way, he has been.

"You told him?"

I shake my head. "He thinks it's something else."

Jones nods. He doesn't ask what this 'something else' is. It doesn't matter what it is.

We both look back out the window.

"When?" he asks.

"I don't know. It may already be done."

Jones laughs. It's a brief sound, and it's not a joyful one, but I can't remember the last time I heard him laugh.

"What?" I ask.

"Is he in love with you?" Jones asks.

I face him. "What? No. Of course not. I think it's because of what happened with his sister. When she killed herself, she was fifteen. Same as me when..." I drift off. Neither of us wants to go down memory lane. "She was pregnant when she did it. I didn't know that."

Jones meets my eyes. He should ask about what I just said, anyone would, anyone but Jones.

"Well, if I know Killian Black, he'll make sure it's not a painless death."

"I guess that's one thing we can count on him for."

For the first time in eight years, Jones reaches out to take my hand. It's tentative at first, but then he curls his fingers around mine and looks down at our joined hands for a long while before looking up at me again. "I'm tired, Cilla."

I study him. He's so calm. So sedate. I've always known Jones to be manic. Maybe he was high all the time and I just never knew it. Or never wanted to see it.

"Okay. I'll let you get some sleep." But that's not what he means. I know that deep inside.

"You shouldn't come here every day."

"What?"

"It's not good for you."

"Jones—"

"I'll be out soon. You can see me then."

"Are you trying to get rid of me?" I'm joking, but I know that's exactly what he's doing the minute the words are out. "Jones?"

Panic makes me clench his hand, but he's already pulling away.

"No. Never that, Cilla."

It's a lie. I know it. I hear it.

Jones smiles and stands. "Killian Black will protect what's his and I don't know if either of you know it, but I think you're his. You'll be safe now."

"What do you mean?"

He shrugs. "Just remember that sometimes the beasts aren't what we think they are. Or who we think they are." He looks so at peace and so knowing that I can't help but watch him as he draws the covers back and lies on the bed. He closes his eyes and I think he's already fallen asleep.

I look at him and I start to cry and can't stop. Just tears falling, falling without sound. I seem to have a never-ending supply of them. I can't help but feel like this is it. This is the last time I'll see him.

"No." I wipe my eyes and shake my head then tuck the blanket up to his chin. "I'll see you soon, Jones." I walk out the door and down the stairs. When I step outside, the air is freezing. It makes me shudder. John, the driver, pulls the car up to the front steps when he sees me. I get in and as we drive away, I glance up to my brother's window where we'd just been. I wonder what our faces looked like up there.

Two lost souls.

Ghosts, really.

Helen delivers a garment bag to me on Saturday afternoon. I haven't seen or heard from Kill in three days now but I guess I'll be seeing him tonight.

Apart from going to the facility to see Jones, I've spent these days in my room with the window open, breathing in chilly air. All I can think about is my brother and how he was before I left the last time. How he fell asleep so quietly. So quickly. How strangely knowing he sounded just before that.

I think about what he said about beasts not being what they appear to be. Who we think they are. I think about his question to me but push that away. I can't think about Kill that way—not as protector, not as lover. I'm his for one month. Just two more weeks to go. That's all. As far as Callahan, I can't think about that either because I don't know what Kill's done, if anything.

Helen tells me the time John will pick me up to drive me into the city. I have an hour so I reluctantly get up and drag myself into the shower. I feel like I'm on auto-pilot as I get ready, putting on makeup, lining my eyes more thickly than usual in darkest black, blow-drying my hair and pinning it into a twist, sweeping my bangs to the side. With fifteen minutes left to go, I unzip the garment bag to find the most beautiful gown I've ever seen inside. It's the color of ashes of roses. I take it out of the bag. It's strapless and floor-length with a high slit on one thigh. Tender flowers and delicate pearls adorn one side of the dress from breast to hip.

I take off the bathrobe I'm wearing and put on the dress. It's a perfect fit, the material hugging my body in the most flattering way. I open the shoe box next, momentarily forgetting my troubles, momentarily feeling like a princess. Inside is a pair of pointy-toe pumps in a shade of champagne to complement the dress. I sit on the bed to put them on and wrap the pretty straps around my ankles. The heels are thin but I stand comfortably and with the additional four inches, the dress just touches the floor.

The last box is gift wrapped in a shade of blue with a white ribbon any woman will recognize. Carefully, I undo the bow and set it aside. I take the lid off the box and find a second box inside. I take it out, brush my fingers over the velvet, open it to find a pair of platinum drop earrings with three diamonds on each.

I put my hand to my mouth. These probably cost more than I make in a month. I take one out, handle it gently as I put it on. I repeat with the other and, keeping my gaze down, I walk to the full-length mirror.

A knock comes on the door. "John is here." It's Helen.

"I'll be right out," I say, before raising my eyes to my reflection, not allowing my gaze to linger there. Not allowing myself to dwell on thoughts of what can't be.

22

KILL

I've been in New York for the last day and a half, but I haven't been able to go back to the house.

Cilla lied to me.

I know the real truth. And it all makes sense. It all makes perfect, sick sense.

But I meant what I said—I'm no hero. I slew her dragon, but I'm not her hero. I can't be.

I step off the elevator and survey the club. It's Mea Culpa's anniversary party. Tonight, the guest list is by invitation only. But it's not the anniversary I'm celebrating. There's a meeting tonight too. An important one. Fuck my timing.

"Killian," Mrs. Borgado lays her hand on my forearm. She's the wife of Bennie Borgado, cousin to the boss of one of the Detroit mob families.

I force a smile, but my eyes are on the door. I'm waiting for Cilla, who's late.

"Mrs. Borgado, you look enchanting." She's in her mid-forties and attractive, but I'm not interested in her.

"Thank you, Killian. It's quite the party you've put on."

"Thank you, Mrs. Borgado."

"Layne. I told you to call me Layne."

"Layne," I say, sipping my drink. The door opens and, just like it has every time it's opened in the last half hour, my heart rate picks up. But it's not her.

The door hasn't quite closed when it's pushed open again. My jaw tightens. I glance at Hugo who sees him at the same time I do. Benji. Fucking Benji crashing this party.

Chrissy runs in behind him.

"Excuse me," I say to Mrs. Borgado, frankly relieved for the excuse to walk away. I meet Chrissy's eye to let her know I've got this and greet my cousin just as he's taking a drink off a passing server's tray. "Ben. What are you doing here?"

"You're having a party and didn't invite me? I'm hurt."

"You're not hurt. You're drunk."

Hugo walks over. "Boss?"

I shake my head. "I got this." I turn Ben away from the group. "What are you doing here, Ben? You knew the club was closed for a private party."

"I got scared. What I told you the other day. What if they come after me?"

I exhale and it takes all I have not to shake my cousin to death. "I told you I'm not paying off this debt."

He swallows the contents of his glass, glances around nervously. "I need another drink."

The lights go down and the music changes. I check my watch as spotlights illuminate the stages. It's almost time for the meeting and the entertainment has begun. I need to get this idiot out of here.

"No drink. Club's closed tonight."

I signal one of my men over. "Get Ben a taxi."

"Yes, sir."

I have to physically take hold of Ben and walk him toward the exit. "Why? Why's tonight such a big deal?"

"Because I said so." I check my watch. The guest of honor will be here soon.

"Christ, I'll go," he says.

Hugo's beside me in the next minute. Cilla's still not here and I see a couple of men walking into the meeting room.

"I'll take care of this," Hugo says, relieving me of my cousin.

"Kill, what the fuck. We're family—"

I don't bother to answer. Just as Hugo opens the doors to escort my cousin out, Cilla steps into view with John a few steps behind her. I swear every eye in the place turns to the doors when she sweeps in wearing the dress I bought her, looking stunning, more beautiful than I've ever seen her. Her hair is swept off her face and her makeup is heavier than usual and fuck if I don't want to go to her, wrap her in my arms and steal her away. Never let her out of my sight again. Never leave her alone again. Not after Florida.

Her gaze finally falls on me. We stare at each other from across the room and it's so fucking cliché and stupid but something shifts inside me and it's like this instinct to protect, to guard, to rescue—fuck, maybe to be her hero— it's like they take over every fiber of my being and she's all I can see, all I can think about.

I go to her, stop just a foot from her. Her eyes are searching mine, and I know the question she wants to ask. But I don't want to talk about Callahan right now.

Drawing her to stand beside me, I address my comment to John, the driver. "You're late."

"An accident, sir. I took the fastest route I could."

I nod. Dismiss him. Turn to Cilla. "You look beautiful."

"Is it done?" she asks.

I nod once.

She doesn't say a word, just keeps staring up at me and I

want to know what's going on in her head because I can't read her eyes. She's too guarded. Too careful. She's had to be.

A waiter passes with champagne. I stop him. "Get me two whiskeys." I don't want champagne. This isn't a celebration.

"Yes, sir."

Cilla puts her hands over her face, rubs it, then her neck. The waiter returns and I take the tumblers, hand her one. Her hand is trembling when she takes the drink and I watch her swallow it. All of it.

"Easy, Cilla."

"Why?" she looks around, locates a waiter with a tray of full champagne glasses and signals him to come over. I watch her. "Get me a bottle," she says, then points to me. "On him so make it a good one."

"Cilla."

"Sir?" the waiter asks me as my cell phone rings. I ignore the call and the look I give him dismisses him, but not before Cilla swallows what's in the glass and takes another from his tray. She turns to face me and gives me a ridiculous smile.

"I'm celebrating," she says, holding the glass up. "To justice. Cheers." She swallows what's in there too.

People are looking now. I take her by the arm, turn her away. "What the fuck is wrong with you?" My phone starts up again. "Jesus!" I take it out and, without looking at the screen, silence it, shove it back into my pocket.

"What's wrong with me? Nothing. I'm the happiest woman in the world tonight. Look at me. All of this?" She spins around, stumbles. I catch her. "A very expensive gift from my dragon slayer." She turns in search of a waiter. I force her attention back to me. "My hero," she adds on, the sarcasm in her tone biting.

Hugo walks toward us. "Santa Maria's here." He gestures to the entrance. It's Giovanni Santa Maria, Dominic Benedetti's cousin, and the second most powerful man on the east coast. He's standing in for Dominic tonight. This is why Ben had to go. This meeting tonight, it's secret. A new alliance is being formed. One that will rock organized crime in North America.

Giovanni scans the room. I've only seen him once before. He's a big guy, as big as me. He's dressed elegantly in an expensive suit and two men flank him. Soldiers. I get the feeling he can handle whatever the fuck comes his way, though.

I give him a nod when he sees me.

The phone starts to vibrate with a call again. "Fuck."

Cilla tries to pull free. "Let me go. I'm here, like you want. Dressed up like you want. I'll even spread my legs for you later, just like you want."

I tug on her arm. "You're embarrassing yourself, Cilla." I dig the phone out of my pocket.

"I don't care what these people think of me so I must be embarrassing you. Let me go home and you won't have to worry about me doing that ever again."

"I'll take her upstairs," Hugo says.

I look at the screen, not expecting what I'm seeing.

"You won't touch me," Cilla spits back, trying to free herself from me.

When I release her, she stumbles backward, but Hugo catches her. I turn my back and swipe the green bar to answer.

"What?" I bark into the phone.

"Don't fucking turn your back on me!" It's Cilla, but I'm not paying attention to her. Not now.

"When?" I ask. Shit. Fuck. Shit. I take a deep breath in, nod, turn to face Cilla. "We'll be right there."

Hugo's holding her back, but she's not fighting anymore. Her expression changes as she watches my face, watches me disconnect the call.

It's like she knows before I say a word because her big eyes fill up with tears and her lip is trembling.

"Cilla," I start.

A tear rolls down her face. "What?" it's barely a whisper.

I signal to Hugo to release her. "You need to take care of the meeting," I tell him.

"What is it?" she's more panicked now.

I rub the scruff of my jaw. "It's your brother."

"What?" She knows what I'm going to say. I see it in her eyes.

"He tried to hurt himself." Hang himself. Like Ginny. My gut twists, and seeing Cilla double over with an unnatural sound, I know exactly what she's feeling. Fucking exactly. It's like the fucking past just catapulted itself into the present because it's not done with me yet. It's not done with either of us.

"He's alive," I say, but I don't know if he's okay. "Let's go."

She straightens, nods. Her face is the color of ashes and there's a strange look in her eyes, a resignation almost. I think this is worse than hysteria.

We're almost out the door when Cilla stops, grips my arm. I look down at her. I already know what she is going to ask. "Is he going to be okay?"

"I don't know."

23

CILLA

I remember what Jones said to me the last time I was here. How he acted so strange. It was as though when I told him that Kill knew about Callahan, that he'd murder him, he was freed of something, something too heavy to bear. Like he could finally rest.

All these years I've thought I've been watching out for Jones, but maybe he's been watching out for me. I don't know any longer who's on more shaky ground, me or him. I don't know who was—is—more damaged.

Maybe there aren't degrees of damage, though. Maybe we're all just clinging to the buoy, any buoy, just managing to keep our noses out of the water. Maybe it's a matter of who went under more. Who took in too much water, too much for there to be any room left for breath. For life.

Jones is lying in a hospital bed in a different room than the one he was in. He has too many tubes attached to him to count. His skin is pale and his lips have lost any color. He looks like a ghost under a sheet. How much weight has he lost these last weeks? The beeping of the machines is overwhelming, they seem to muffle everything else, the other machines, the doctor talking to Kill. Kill's angry words.

I pull the chair closer and sit beside my brother's bed. It's a clear night and the moon shines its silvery light through the large bay window. It's an almost unnatural light. It feels like we're in a space between worlds. Like he's already left this one.

His arms are above the sheet and, with my hand trembling, I reach out to touch his fingers, slowly gather them into mine. I feel the tickle of a tear sliding down my face but I don't move to wipe it away. Instead, I look at him, his face. Feel his cold skin beneath mine.

I knew this was coming the other day.

I knew it the moment he took my hand. It was the first time we'd touched each other since we left Callahan's house. I'd been sixteen. Callahan arranged for Jones to have legal guardianship of me. That was part of the deal. Do as we were told and in time, we would be free. Don't and Callahan would hold on to me once Jones was out. Jones wouldn't be there to protect me anymore. And if Jones told, who'd believe him when Judge Callahan was an upstanding citizen? A man who took in those no one else wanted?

I moved out of Jones's apartment when I turned seventeen. Got a job, supported myself. I think we were both relieved to be apart, although we were never far from each other. Jones tried to put more distance between us with all the moves, but I always followed with the excuse of watching out for him. Saying that he needed me. He didn't need me, though. He needed to be away from me because I know every time he looked at me, he saw what we did. That was one thing I was better at than him. I could block it. I did it while it was happening. I did it when I left. It's like it wasn't me at all.

"Cilla," Kill's hand is on my shoulder.

Startled, I look up at his face.

"One of the nurses forgot something in his room and returned after giving him his medication. It's lucky for him that she did because she found him quickly enough and they were able to cut him down before it was too late."

"So he'll be okay?" The question doesn't fit. I know Jones will never be okay, not like other people.

"He'll survive this without permanent damage, yes."

There's more in the way he doesn't say things than in the words he says. He knows it too. He knows Jones will never really be okay.

"He was lucky," Kill continues. "This time."

I look at him when he adds on that last part. "I'll stay with him. He won't do it again."

"Are you going to watch him 24/7?"

"I can't abandon my brother."

"He's heavily sedated, Cilla. He may need to be—"

"I won't abandon my brother," I repeat more slowly.

"He needs a different sort of care than you can provide."

He's right, I know, but it still feels like abandonment, and I can't face that right now. Instead, I rise to my feet. Face Kill.

"You did this," I say.

"What?"

"You did it. It's because of you. All of this happened because of you."

His eyes narrow, but inside them, I still see pity. Fucking pity. Now, after everything.

"Get out," I say, planting my hands on his chest, attempting to shove him.

"You're in shock—"

"Get the fuck out of my brother's room!"

The doctor says something, walks toward us, but Kill

puts his hand up to stop him without ever taking his eyes from me.

"I'll call the police," I say. "Tell them about our contract. Tell them about your business." I shove again, this time, he captures my wrists. "Get out. Right now."

"I can't help you if you don't let me," he says, but his calm is a thin façade.

"I don't want your help. I never asked for it and neither did he!"

"You did ask for it," he reminds me.

"So this is my fault?"

"No, it's no one's fault, but you can't put your life on permanent hold to help your brother and that's exactly what you'd be doing if you think you could handle this yourself."

I try to pull free, but can't. "Let me go."

He watches me, and I want to know what he sees, what he thinks, but he doesn't let on. Just keeps hold of me and all those damn machines are too loud. Too fucking loud. And it's like he knows it'll only be another minute, another second, before I break down again because that's all I can seem to do these days. All I can do around him unless I fight him. There's no in-between for us. He knows the truth. I see it in his eyes. He learned it when he went to get my pound of flesh.

"Cilla," he says, a hint of tenderness in the way he says it.

"Stop. Let me help you."

I shake my head, drop my gaze, but his words, God how I want to say yes. How I want to melt into his strong arms, let him hold me. Keep me.

Hide me.

"Cilla." The way he's holding me changes. He pulls me to him, or tries but, but I can't. I can't want this. Can't have it.

It's too hard and I want to go back to the way it was before. Before I asked for his help. Before he found out.

A machine starts to beep. I turn, we both do, and a team of doctors and nurses rushes in.

"You need to go," one of them says.

"No!" They're calling out orders, words that don't make sense to me. I can't see my brother anymore.

"You need to take her outside," someone says again.

Kill nods, takes me by the arm and forces me out.

"What happening?" I'm frantic, but Kill won't let me go. He just keeps holding me, keeps pulling me into his chest, keeps petting my hair, trying to soothe me.

The frantic sounds from the room quiet a few moments later. That's when Kill loosens his hold on me, let's me turn toward the door. He's still got my wrist and won't let go.

"Let's sit down," Kill says. He doesn't wait for me to reply but walks us to the chairs down the hall.

I don't know how long we sit there, but I can hear the beeps come regularly now. If it was a bad sign, they'd come to tell us. They'd come right away. I just keep my eyes on the door of Jones's room for I don't know how long until, finally, a doctor steps out.

"He's stable again," he says. He's watching us cautiously.

I breathe a sigh of relief, try again to pull free. "I want to see him."

The doctor and Kill exchange a look, before the doctor turns to me. "I don't think that's a good idea right now, Ms. Hawking. Your brother can hear what's going on. I'm certain of it. And he's in a very delicate state right now."

"What do you mean?"

"I mean he can be upset very easily. I think it's best if you go home."

"Go home?" I turn back to find Kill watching us. I realize

he moves his hand so he's no longer gripping my wrist but holding my hand. "I don't understand," I tell the doctor.

"He'll be okay, we'll pull him through this, but he needs some time to heal."

"Without me." It's not a question. I'm Jones's poison. What happened...he sees it every time he sees me.

"Cilla," Kill starts. "I'll bring you back in a few days."

"I think that's best, Mr. Black."

"You'll call me with hourly updates," Kill says.

"Yes, sir."

"Good." Kill turns me to face him, takes my shoulders, rubs them, squeezes a little until I look up at him. "He's going to be okay. Let's give him some time. Space."

I shake my head, but I'm powerless.

"Come on, Cilla."

I let him walk me down the hall, out the front doors. He doesn't speak as he sets me in the SUV, straps me in. He doesn't start the car right away but checks messages on his phone, talks to Hugo. I'm not really listening, though. Instead, I look out into the fields Jones and I were watching just a few days ago. There's no traffic on the lonely road beyond.

When he hangs up, we pull out of the parking lot.

"Where are we going?"

"I need to stop by the club. Pick something up. We can stay at the penthouse tonight so we'll be closer."

I lean my head back, close my eyes for a minute. "He wouldn't have done this if I hadn't told him what you were going to do to Callahan."

"You can't know that. Jones is in a bad place. He's detoxing and maybe for the first time in his life, he's facing what happened. Or being forced to."

The unspoken fact that he knows everything sits in the

car with us, taking up too much space, not leaving any for me.

"This needs to end," I say, facing him.

"You're upset. We'll talk about it later."

"No. Not later. Now."

He sighs, turns to me, squeezes my knee in warning. "Later. And we're not talking about ending anything. We're talking about what I learned."

I swallow. He studies me and his eyes, it's like they penetrate to my core. He knows everything. I shift my gaze to my lap. I can't do this. I can't talk about what happened. I need out. I need away from him.

Traffic picks up as we near the city, take the turnoff to the club. The parking lot is empty but for one car. I check the time and realize it's been hours since we left the party. I thought it had been minutes.

Kill makes a sound when he sees it. It's a low, displeased growl. He parks beside the car, switches off the engine, turns to me.

"Stay here. I'll be back in a few minutes."

"Are you afraid you won't have the remaining weeks you're owed?" I ask.

He blinks, looks confused. "What?"

I have to say it. Enrage him. Wound him. "That's what it is, isn't it? You're afraid you won't have access 24/7 to the pussy you're owed? That's why you won't let me go?"

He fists his hands and I can see the anger creeping into his face.

"I've hit the nail on the head, huh?" I keep going, goading him, because it's the only way I know how to deal with this.

"No, Cilla, that's not it."

"Then let me go."

He shakes his head, rubs his jaw, runs that hand through his hair. It sticks up when he does, dark spikes on top of his head. "It's been a really long night."

"For me too. A long two weeks."

He takes the key out of the ignition and opens his door. "I'll be back. Stay here."

I climb out too, follow him, my heels echoing in the empty night. "You don't hear me, do you? You don't hear anything but what you want."

We reach the side door and he chooses a key from the ring in his hand, turns to me. "I heard *and saw* plenty at Callahan's," he says.

It's like a hit to the gut. I clutch my belly, stumble backward, feel my face burn, feel shame spread its icy darkness through me.

"Shit. Cilla, that's not—"

I look down, grip the railing to keep upright. "I need some water." And to disappear from here. From his sight.

It takes him a moment, but he slides the key into the lock, then stops because the door isn't locked. "Fucking Benji."

24

KILL

Fuck. I don't need this right now. I don't need to deal with Ben right fucking now. I wish I could take her straight back to Rockcliffe House and lock her away until this passes. Until she's thinking straight again. But I need to pick something up. Hugo will have left it for me and I need it out of the office. I can't take a chance it'll be found.

Cilla's on the verge of a breakdown. I feel it. She knows I know, but she won't face the fact. I'm going to need to make her face it.

Callahan didn't suffer enough before he died. Not nearly. What I saw at his house was sick. Sicker than I had thought. Sicker than I imagined possible.

She hadn't lied when she'd told me he didn't rape her, but I already knew that. He raped her brother. Knew that too. What I didn't know was what that pervert made them do. The sick bastard recorded everything. Every single sick moment.

Thing is, he'd been abusing kids for years. He had a pattern, like Hugo had learned, and when he was through with the kids, when the boy was old enough to leave the house, he'd promise to release the girl in exchange for silence. But for kids who are abused like that for that long, you don't need to make deals for them to keep your secret. Shame will do that for you. Shame and self-hatred. Because they think they're accomplices.

I look at Cilla and she can't look at me. I try to touch her, but she jumps back. I don't push. "Let's go in. It's cold out here."

She nods, keeps her head down, walks in.

I wonder how long Ben's had a key to the club. How long he's been waiting to get in here when Hugo or I aren't here. I guess Hugo went home with a girl tonight and maybe Ben found his opportunity. What I want to know is when the fuck did he even get a key to get in here? I'm done with this asshole.

I walk into the dark main floor of the building, switch on a light. Look around. But there's no one here.

"Whose car is that?" Cilla asks, sensing my mood. "Who's here?"

At the elevator, I punch in the code and the doors slide open.

"My cousin." I'm getting more and more pissed off by the minute. If he's not down here, that means he's up in my office. That means he's watched me punch in the code, memorized it. Of all the nights he cannot be in my office, this is it.

Although maybe he's been there before tonight.

But I stop short. I realize I don't want her up there, not if he's there. Because maybe I underestimated him all along. Maybe this isn't about twenty grand at all.

I walk around the nearest bar, get a bottle of water out of the refrigerator, open it. "Stay here while I handle this."

She nods, takes a seat on the stool where I set the bottle

of water. She doesn't drink. Instead, she hugs her coat to herself like she's cold, and her eyes are far away.

I don't want to leave her alone right now, but I need to take care of this.

"I'll be down as soon as I can."

She seems to shrink into herself.

I give Cilla one more glance as the doors close. It's a short ride up and as soon as the doors slide open and I hear what I hear, all the things I'm feeling take on a different form. Rage. Pure, unfiltered rage.

Cilla. Cilla that night I recorded her.

I almost don't see Ben for the red.

My fingernails dig into my palms at the sight of my cousin sitting behind my desk, the dim light of the lamp illuminating him. He moves into that light, eyes not on the monitor but on me, the look in them vengeful, ugly. Full of hate.

This is Ben. This is the real Ben. And I've been closing my eyes to it all along.

I switch on the lights.

Ben stands. He looks shocked to see me.

His face is covered in bruises, one eye swollen nearly shut, his lip cut. Blood is crusted on his ripped shirt. But when I see what he's holding in his hand, I know this wasn't ever about money. There was no twenty grand debt.

"What the fuck is wrong with you, Ben?" I take a step toward him but stop when he raises a shaky hand, in it the pistol I keep in my desk. I really need to lock that drawer.

"What are you doing in my office?" But I know when I watch him slip the thing he's holding into his pocket.

"I told you they'd come after me," he says.

When he talks, I notice one of his front teeth is broken.

"I fucking told you!" he yells.

"What did you put in your pocket, Ben?"

He's jittery. Anxious. His eyes wide. I can't tell if he's stoned or scared. Maybe both.

"Nothing," he says.

He's a bad liar. "Put the gun down. You don't want to hurt yourself."

"Fuck you. You're not the only one who knows how to use a goddamned gun."

I take another step. I need to disarm this fool before he does something stupid. "Put the fucking gun down, Ben."

"Don't you mean Benji?" he spits. "I'm tired of you and your goon calling me that."

"Jesus Christ." I shake my head, walk to the bar, get a bottle of whiskey.

"Don't fucking move!"

Ignoring him, I pour a tumbler. Turn to face him. Drink a sip before setting it down. I've got another pistol stashed behind the bar, but if things go that far, this will be the last night of Benji's life, and that's not what I want.

"I'm going to ask you nicely one more time to put the gun down." The sound of Cilla coming over and over again is gnawing at me. "And turn that off."

He grins, cocks his head to the side. "What? You got a soft spot for Jones's sister."

I take two steps. He takes a small one back, but the chair is behind him so he's trapped between it and my desk and his eyes are bouncing between the elevator door and the locked one to the stairwell.

"Turn. It. Off." I squint to get a better look at him. I'm blocking his way to either exit—he won't be leaving here until I get what he put in his pocket back. "Antonino's men do that to you?" I ask, not that I give a fuck, although I realize he's never been properly beaten before. My bad. I should have taken Hugo's advice and done it years ago. I've been coddling him and he's taken that for weakness. I made a fucking traitor out of him.

"They're not done with me."

"What did you put in your pocket, Ben?"

"Nothing."

"Did you agree to the beating? Make this look more real in case I walked in on you? Or is that a sample of what they'll do to you if you don't give them what you're stealing from me?"

He starts fidgeting, shifting his weight.

"Are you stoned, Ben?"

He cocks the gun.

I take a deep breath in, exhale slowly, watch him. "Turn that off, put the gun down and we'll talk. Last chance."

He gives me a nervous chuckle. "I'm the one holding the fucking—"

I lunge at him, ducking down as I do so when he pulls the trigger, the bullet flies over my head and shatters a bottle of something before lodging into the wall. Knocking Ben down isn't hard. He's not a big guy and liquor has only weakened him. We knock the chair over on its side as I take him to the ground, wrestle the gun from him, and slide it across the floor.

"What the fuck is wrong with you?" I ask again, taking him by the collar and dragging him up as I rise to my feet. I sit his ass down on the couch, pick up the pistol and set it on the corner of my desk, then turn my attention to the computer. I find the file that contains the recording of Cilla and hit delete.

From the corner of my eye, I see Ben rise to his feet, take a step toward the bar.

I turn to him. "Sit your ass back down."

He looks at me, fear in his bloodshot eyes. He sits.

I fold my arms across my chest. "What do you think you're doing here? In *my* office, behind *my* desk, on *my* computer. Aiming my own gun at me?"

He scratches his head, shifts his gaze to the glass of whiskey I'd just poured that's still sitting on the bar. The bottle is what shattered. It was nearly full and fucking expensive.

"Last chance to tell me what you put in your pocket."

"I told you they'd come after me," he says again.

"Antonino?"

He nods.

I hold out my hand. "Give me what you took and I'll protect you."

His eyes narrow. "You weren't supposed to record it, were you?"

He's talking about the meeting. He knew all along what was going down tonight. And no, I wasn't supposed to record it, but fuck that. This is my club. My rules. No exceptions.

"I just don't get one thing. Are you working for Antonino or are you really scared?" I ask.

"Fuck you," he says, and bolts up, tries to dash past me. I grab him easily, hold him by the throat and dig out the thumb drive from his pocket. Tossing him back on the couch as I slip it into my pocket.

"You don't know what they'll do to me if I don't give them that drive."

I snort. "You're pathetic, you know that? Go home. Get the fuck out of my sight before I hurt you."

"What home? I don't have a fucking home. Remember, you took it!"

"I took what?"

"Rockcliffe House. This club. My father. Everything."

I'm out of patience. "Rockcliffe House belonged to my mother. It never belonged to the Black family. You and your father lived there because when my father died and that asshole father of yours was granted custody of Ginny and me, it made the most fucking sense. When your father raped my sister, he signed his own death warrant. Ginny was a kid. He fucking raped her, Ben."

He knows this, I know he does.

"This club I built from the ground up," I continue. "You have no part in it."

"You fund it with drug money."

"That's not any of your fucking business."

"And now you've got it all, huh?" His expression changes, his eyes narrow, he leans back almost looking relaxed. "The house. The club. The status. The pretty girl."

Something about the way he says that last part bugs me.

"Wouldn't it be a shame if even one of those things were to be taken away." He says the words *taken away* with special emphasis, his teeth gnashed together, like it's a threat.

I'm still processing when he continues.

"What's the matter? For the first time in our lives, have I got the last word, Cous?" he asks, standing.

I hear the elevator doors slide open then. Surprised I turn toward it. Find Cilla standing there, her eyes wide as saucers.

I take a step to her. "What are you doing?"

She looks from me to Ben. "I heard—"

Before she can finish, Ben leaps toward the desk, grabs the gun. I whirl around as he raises his arm, aiming the weapon at Cilla, cocking it. She screams at the same instant as the gun fires, as I tackle him to the ground, close my hand around his, the one that's holding the weapon. But he's cocked it again and it's pressing against my chest. I manage to move just as it goes off once more, ripping flesh apart, sending blood and tissue against the walls, the desk, the carpet.

I fall backward as I hear Cilla scream. I look to my shoulder, my jacket is shredded, there's a deep gash in the skin beneath. It burns like fucking hell and when I turn to Ben, he's staring at it too, like he's more shocked than anyone.

"Give me the fucking gun," I say, not waiting for him to comply but taking it from him. He falls backward, he doesn't even put up a fight. I stand, empty it of bullets and put it in the waistband of my pants.

"I'm sorry. Fuck. I'm sorry."

"Stop your fucking rambling." I look at Cilla who's pressed against the far wall. She's staring at the wound in my arm. I go to her. "Are you hurt?" She can't seem to drag her eyes from the mess of my shoulder. I look her over, she's not hurt. Just in shock. "You should have stayed downstairs."

I pull my phone out from inside my pocket, dial Hugo. He answers.

"Where the fuck are you?" I bark into the phone.

"Just pulling in. Fuck." He must see Ben's car.

"My office. Now." I disconnect the call, take Cilla to the couch, sit her down. "Stay."

"You're bleeding."

"It's fine." I turn to Benji who's managed to get to his feet and is cowering in the corner. I go to him, take him by the collar of his shirt.

"How dare you come in here threatening me in *my own club*, with my own fucking gun? How dare you threaten *my girl*? Aim a fucking gun at her?"

"Cous—Kill, please."

"Did you watch it?" I ask, referring to what I know is on the USB stick.

I know he did from the look in his eyes.

"Fuck." The elevator doors close, then a few minutes later, open again with Hugo. He steps inside, looks around.

"Take him downstairs." I need to figure out what to do with him.

Hugo moves.

"No! Get off me! You can't do this!" Ben yells.

Hugo drags him out. The doors close, leaving me with Cilla. She's staring at me wide-eyed, her mouth open. She looks a mess, what's left of her makeup is smeared, her hair half out of its twist, my blood on her dress.

I realize I called her 'my girl' but she isn't that. She never was.

She could have been hurt tonight. Or worse. Her brother is lying in a hospital bed attached to too many machines after trying to kill himself. Is she better off for knowing me? Or is she in danger because of it? Is she a target for my enemies?

I rub my face. My neck. I know what I have to do. There's only one thing.

"Are you...are you going to hurt him?" she asks.

I don't answer. What I need to do to Ben is separate of this. Separate of her. And if I wasn't sure before, I am now.

"You're free," I say.

She looks at me, confused. "What?"

"I'm releasing you from your contract. You're free."

"I don't—"

But I think of something. "With one condition." She stands. I go to her. "You stay away from The Black Swan."

I'm not breathing. Not blinking. I need to memorize her now because I have to let her go. I can't ever see her again.

When the elevator doors open again, Hugo steps into my office.

I drag my eyes from Cilla. "Take her to her apartment. We're done here."

Before anyone can speak, before I can change my mind, I step onto the elevator and I don't look back when the doors close. I don't look back when I'm downstairs or when I walk through the main room. Not when I step out into the bitterly cold, clear night and get to my car. It's once I'm there I stop. I take a deep breath in, have to force it because the weight pushing against my chest doesn't leave room for air. I force myself to move, to get in the car. To start the engine. To drive. I'm on autopilot, I can't think. I drive. I head back to Rockcliffe House without her.

Without her.

25

CILLA

All I can do is stare at Kill's back as he steps onto the elevator.

He gave me what I wanted. Exactly what I asked for. So why do I feel like someone's just knocked the wind out of me?

"Ready?" Hugo breaks the silence. How could I have forgotten a man his size was in the room?

"Y...yes."

He punches in the code, which I know from when Kill used it earlier to come upstairs, and we step onto the elevator. He doesn't touch me and I take one last look around the office, at the blood splattered on every surface. Think about how Ben raised the gun and aimed it at me. How Kill took the bullet instead and saved my life.

The doors slide closed. It's an awkward ride down and, chilled, I hug my coat to myself. I don't speak and barely breathe and Hugo escorts me outside and into a car—his, I presume—and we drive through the bitterly cold night to my apartment. He walks me upstairs. Unlocks my door. Enters it before me, walking through each of the rooms, turning on all of the lights, before setting my key on the counter and turning to leave. He doesn't speak a word as he does all of this. He barely glances at me.

Once he's gone, I snap out of my daze. I pick up the key, lock the door. Lean my back against it.

This place feels foreign. How can that be after only a few weeks? Even the smell is no longer familiar. I take off my coat and let it fall to the floor. My shoes come off next. Then the dress. The panties. I'm not wearing a bra. I leave it all as I go into my bedroom, switching off lights on my way.

I wonder what would have happened tonight if Jones hadn't done what he'd done. I can't bring myself to say the words.

When I get to the full-length mirror in my room, I stand before it. I'm naked but for the earrings. I wonder if he'll want those back. I take each one off slowly, set them down on the nightstand. I'll send them back to the club tomorrow.

Tomorrow.

But what if he changes his mind and comes for me?

He won't. I know he won't. And the strange thing is, that's the part that terrifies me. I won't ever see Killian Black again.

I follow the trail the tear that's sliding down my face leaves. It's a smear of pink where blood has dried on my cheek. His blood.

He took a bullet for me.

He called me his girl.

But I'm not that anymore. Was I ever?

I'm very tired suddenly. Like I can't stay on my feet a moment longer. I draw the covers on my bed back. It should feel familiar, but it doesn't. It's like I'm lying in a stranger's bed. What's happened to me in the last two weeks?

So much.

So fucking much.

I close my eyes. I want to shut everything out just for a few hours. I want to forget just for a little while. I entertain the thought of amnesia again. The hope of it. It's useless, I know. Fantasy.

When I wake up the next morning, I don't feel any better. In fact, it's like I didn't sleep twelve hours straight. I'm so tired and heavy, I can barely drag myself out of bed and into the bathroom to shower. I stand under the water for a long time watching water pool at my feet. It's pink at first. I didn't realize how much blood was on me, in my hair. I should change the sheets. I should do a lot of things. But I can only manage to dress myself and sit on the couch with the phone in my hand.

I dial the Dover Recovery Center and talk to a nurse there. I think she's the one who was there the first day I'd gone in because she seems to recognize me.

"How is my brother doing?"

"He's awake, woke up early this morning."

"But how is he?"

She sighs. "The doctor is in with him now. Shall I ask him to call you after his meeting?"

"Yes. Please." I give her the number of the landline and wonder where my purse is. Where my cell phone is. As I hang up and as if on cue, the doorbell rings. My heart races as I go to answer, not sure who I expect to find, but still surprised when a courier is standing there with a box.

"Priscilla Hawking?"

"Yes."

"Sign here."

Absently, I do. I then take the box and he leaves. Inside, I find my laptop, my purse, wallet. Nothing else though. I'm not sure what I expect there to be. What would there be? A fucking note?

I stand and decide instead of waiting for the doctor to call me, I'll go see Jones myself. I'll have to make some arrangements with them anyway. Neither Jones nor I can afford a place like that and I'll assume they'll want him out once they figure that out.

When I get outside, I realize my car must still be at Jones's apartment. I grab a taxi and take it there, and find it in exactly the place I'd parked that night and soon, I'm outside the Dover Recovery Center. I head inside and decide to bypass the reception desk but as I take a few steps down the hall, I'm greeted by the same nurse as the first time Kill brought me here. She seems surprised to see me.

"Ms. Hawking?"

I stop. Turn. "Yes?"

"Didn't Dr. Moore call you?"

"Oh, maybe." I had given him the landline. "I'm here though and I'd like to see my brother."

"Just a minute please. I'll call the doctor to come talk with you."

"What? Why?"

She looks almost embarrassed and a moment later, two men come around the corner discussing a file.

"Oh, there he is. Dr. Moore?" The nurse is visibly relieved.

I recognize the doctor and he recognizes me. He closes the file, excuses himself from the other man and heads toward us.

"Ms. Hawking, I left a message."

"I didn't get it. I'd left the house. What's going on? Is Jones okay?"

"He's fine. Let's go into my office, shall we?"

"Where's Jones?" I ask, refusing to budge until he tells me.

"He's in the same room as last night and he's with a nurse."

"Okay." I follow him into his office which is small but neat. I sit. "What's going on?"

He takes a deep breath in. "Jones has finally opened up about things."

I clear my throat, look away for a moment.

"I think it's in his best interest if you give him some time to work through this."

"Time?"

"Ms. Hawking, I think it'll be damaging for him to see you right now. He feels quite protective of you, and at the same time..." he trails off as if searching for the words, but I don't want to hear it. I can guess.

"He doesn't want to see me?" I can't push this. I don't want to because in a way, I understand.

"His mental condition is...fragile. I know it's not what you want to hear, but my priority is my patient. Please understand."

"When then? How long until I can see him?"

"Give it a few weeks. I'll stay in touch with you. Mr. Black has asked me to keep you apprised of Jones's progress."

My heart leaps at the mention of his name. The doctor clears his throat and opens a file.

"Mr. Black is providing for the best possible care, Ms. Hawking."

"What do you mean?"

He looks confused. "I mean he's hired the best doctors."

"Jones and I, we can't afford..."

He puts his hand up. "Mr. Black is taking care of the expenses." He checks his watch. "Now if you'll excuse me?"

I rise. "You'll call me…"

"Daily."

I shake his extended hand, although I'm still uncertain.

"Thank you for understanding."

I walk out of the building feeling deflated. It's a blustery day, clear and windy, truly winter, and it looks like snow is coming. I get to my car, look back at the room I think is his with the big bay window. I'm tempted to go back inside and see him just once, but I understand what the doctor said. Why he said it. Jones needs time away from me. I've known it for a long time.

26

CILLA

The next four weeks creep slowly past without incident. I still haven't seen Jones although his doctor does call me daily, as promised. Kill kept his word. I'm free from my contract. I half expected him—wanted him—to come back for me, to change his mind and forcefully take me back to Rockcliffe House, but he hasn't. I haven't seen him or anyone associated with him.

In fact, it's almost like those two weeks didn't happen at all.

Almost.

Except that I can't forget them. Can't forget how they made me feel. How *he* made me feel. And I can't help but wonder if he walked away because of what he found out when he went to Florida. Because he said as much, didn't he? Not only heard but saw.

The news reported Judge Callahan's disappearance three weeks ago, but the story isn't a headliner anymore. People move on. They forget. At least these sort of things, they do.

Turned out Kill was right about one thing. It doesn't

make a difference to know that he's dead. That he suffered when he died. It doesn't make any difference at all because the dragons, they're inside us. Inside me and Jones.

Having mine slain didn't make a difference in the end.

Almost having a hero didn't matter.

Almost doesn't matter.

I shut the lid of my laptop and look around my dark apartment. I can't work. I haven't been able to since everything happened. I think about Jones and wish I could talk to him. Just hear from him that he's okay. Even though I know it's for his own good, it still hurts to stay away.

It's late and I didn't bother to turn on any lights. The sounds of the city fill my apartment and street light filters in from between the slats of the blinds. I get up, go to my bedroom, switch on the lights there.

Tonight, I'm going to go through with it.

Tonight, I'm going to take back my power. My control.

Tonight I'm going to put Killian Black out of my mind, even if it means breaking the one condition he gave me.

From inside my closet, I find one of the dresses I used to wear when I went to The Black Swan. After stripping, I put it on and look at my reflection. The little pink dress is too short and too tight. Too cheap. It exposes too much of me. It says that I'm available. That I'm on the prowl.

I pull my hair into a ponytail and apply makeup. Heavy makeup with dark lipstick. The makeup, too, matches the dress. It sends the same message.

Not bothering with stockings, I slip on a pair of fuck me pumps. They hurt my feet, but I need that too right now. I don't stare too long at my reflection. I don't want to do this but I have to. This is the only way I'll be free of him. I just need to go back to the way things were. To a time before him.

I put on a long coat and head out to my car, which is parked around the corner. This is the third time I'm going to The Black Swan, except that this time, I'm determined to enter the bar. The last two times I turned around and drove back home. Like I'm keeping my end of the bargain. My promise to him. Tonight though, I'm going through with this. My time with Kill is up anyway. He can't expect me to never fuck again. I'm sure he doesn't care at all who I fuck, actually. If he did, he wouldn't have walked away.

I arrive too quickly and I have to force myself to get out of the car. The parking lot is full and lights flicker inside the building. It's run down, outside and in, the wood looking like it'll collapse at any time and maybe that's part of the appeal for me. I get to the doors, pull one open. I'd forgotten how the scent of cigarette smoke mixed with that of cheap whiskey. How it clung to your clothes and hair for days.

I see the eyes that turn my way when I step inside. Scanning the room for my prey, I make my way to an empty stool at the bar. That's how I look at the men here. Prey. That's all. They will serve a purpose. Feed my need.

"Whiskey neat," I order, not sure why because I'm not a whiskey drinker, but tonight, when the bartender sets the chipped glass in front of me and pours, I swallow it all and signal for a second.

The liquid burns my throat. It's not like Kill's whiskey. The burn of the good stuff is different. But that doesn't matter. I swivel around in my seat, lean my back against the bar. As I scan the eyes of the many men here, I zero in on one. A tall, blond, and not so handsome stranger.

He's standing against the wall with one hand in his pocket, the other holding a half-full beer. He raises his glass when he sees me looking.

I cock my head to the side. Finish my drink. Stand.

I'm still wearing my coat, but I unbutton it, slide it off as I turn and walk toward the bathrooms. I don't have to look back to know he's following.

The ladies room door opens and a woman stumbles out, gives me a nasty once over as she lets the door drop rather than passing it to me. She can go fuck herself. I enter, go to the farthest stall. It's the biggest one.

I hear the door open behind me and I turn to find the man standing there awkwardly.

Reaching into my pocket, I take out a condom.

I feel a little queasy to do it, but this is why I came. This is how I'll take back what I gave to Kill.

He gives me an uneasy smile.

I set the condom on the counter. "Don't tell me you've never done this before," I taunt, then push into the bathroom stall and reach under my dress to take off my panties, but I can't.

Footsteps follow. I hear the ripping of the package. I take a deep breath in, try to calm myself.

What the fuck am I doing? This isn't what I want. It's not the same. It's not—

But the stall door opens and the stranger stands there looking me over. When he grins, I think he needs braces. He undoes his belt, pulls it apart, unbuttons his pants. Beige pants with a stain on one thigh. Mustard maybe.

I shake my head. This isn't what I want.

"No."

"What do you mean, no?"

I push past him, but he catches me. "I change my mind," I say with as much strength as I can muster, realizing for the first time in all the years I've been doing this how dangerous it is. How lucky I've been.

"Hold on there, sweetheart—"

Sweetheart.

"Don't call me that."

He's licking his lips and he's too close, too disgustingly close.

"Let go of me."

But he doesn't release my wrist while sliding his other hand down my hip, up my thigh.

"Don't touch me!" I shove against him, but he's big and he's not as drunk as I thought earlier.

"You got me all worked up," he says, hiking my dress up. "You want it rough? That what it is?" He spins me around, shoves me painfully against the wall, shoves my dress to my waist.

"Let me go!" His dirty hand covers my mouth and I hear him unzip his pants, hear his breathing change when his fingers slide into the waistband of my panties. "No! Stop!"

The bathroom door slams open then and before I know it, someone pulls him off me. I turn to face the room just as the back of the man's head crashes into the mirror over top of the sink, shattering it. With a scream, I turn my back as shards rain down.

"She said stop, you fucking asshole." It's Kill. He's here. When the man slides sideways from the counter, Kill draws him up by the collar. "What part of no didn't you understand, dickhead?"

The man doesn't even get a single hit in. Kill is pummeling him, his fury fierce, out of control.

"Kill, stop!" I'm calling out, trying to drag him off. "It's enough! It's enough!"

Hugo walks in then, gives me a look. I realize then why no one has busted into the bathroom because they have to hear what's going on.

Kill straightens, turns his angry gaze to me. "Did he hurt you?"

I shake my head no.

"Good." He turns to Hugo. "Take this asshole out back and make sure he learns a lesson."

Hugo is already dragging him away and Kill takes a step toward me.

I back up, the violence in his eyes frightening.

"I gave you one condition," he says, looking me over from head to toe. I realize my dress is still bunched around my waist when he tugs it roughly down.

"I...the four weeks—"

"Bullshit. I didn't put an expiration date on it."

I'm backed against the wall and he's got me trapped.

"This is dangerous, Cilla. These men—"

"Are dangerous? Like you?"

"I'm not dangerous to you."

"You're the worst for me."

He cups my chin, forces me to look up as he searches my face. I do the same. I've missed him. I've missed him so much.

"What were you doing?" he asks, the look in his eyes no longer angry but something else. Something tender.

"Taking back control. I thought."

He shakes his head. "What made you come in this time?"

"How did you know?" I ask.

"I've had men on you."

"You've been watching me?" He doesn't reply. I shake my head. "You always liked watching, didn't you? You install cameras in my apartment too? Sorry it's been such a snore."

What I say has obviously annoyed him because he takes

my arm roughly and walks me toward the door. "Let's go. We're done here."

"I'm not done here!" I dig my heels in.

He stops. "You *are* done here. For good."

"You can't do this."

"Like hell I can't. I change my mind."

"What?"

He gives me a wicked grin, and before I know it, he hoists me up over his shoulder and smacks my ass hard.

"Ow!"

He walks through the door, into the bar which is remarkably quiet all of a sudden. "I said I change my mind. I don't release you from your contract. I'm taking you back, in fact."

A cold gust of air hits the backs of my thighs when we step outside. Hugo comes around the corner rubbing the knuckles of one hand, and I get the feeling he sees everything even when he doesn't seem to be looking at anything particular at all.

We reach Kill's car and he opens the door. He lowers me down to stand. "You can't just take me."

"Really? Why not? Who's going to stop me?" he asks before shoving me into the backseat and sliding in beside me. Hugo closes the door and Kill turns to me. "I can do whatever I want, Cilla." He watches me intently.

Hugo starts to drive.

"You're self-destructing," he says.

"What do you care? You walked away."

"That bar is filthy. Fucking a limp-dick stranger in a bathroom stall? That's not you."

"You don't know me."

"I know everything about you. I know your deepest, darkest secrets. And I know you need a hero. A dark one."

I stop at that, press the heels of my hands into my eyes. When I pull them away, I find him watching me. This is so fucked up. I'm so fucked up.

"What do you want from me?"

He leans in close, his gaze sweeps over my face, pausing at my mouth for a long minute before returning to my eyes.

"I already told you. I want everything. Every fucking thing."

27

CILLA

I'm sitting beside him but I almost can't believe this is real. It's slowly sinking in, the danger I put myself in. I drop my gaze, wipe my eyes.

I don't know what I'm doing. Everything is so mixed up and I feel more out of control than ever.

"You want to punish yourself. Destroy yourself. I'm not going to let that happen," Kill says.

I thought I was past this. Better off than Jones. I thought I had control over this. But seeing Kill, seeing that look in his eyes, the one that says he knows, he truly knows, it's killing me. I want to hide, but at the same time, I need it. I need him. I need someone to know. To see me.

But the instinct to flee, it's just as powerful.

I know it's stupid, but I reach for the door handle, try it. It's locked but he grabs my wrists anyway. Forces my hands on my lap.

"Just let me go."

"You don't want me to."

"I do! This is kidnapping!"

He grins and it's the Kill I first knew. The wicked one.

Although really, he's only ever been wicked, hasn't he? Even when he's tender?

"You don't. In fact, I'm going to give you exactly what you need, sweetheart."

Sweetheart. Whenever he calls me sweetheart, it's like my insides turn to jelly. The way he says it, it's not tender. He has no intention to use it that way. No, with him, it's ownership. I'm his. Again.

I register the rest of his words then, take in the dark, intense burning of his eyes.

"What does that mean?" I ask.

"You're not looking for a hero to save you, Cilla. You're looking for someone dark. You're so fucking lost in there, you can't even see the light to get out. I'm going to come in there and get you. That's what that means."

I shudder at his words, have no response. I sit quietly as we drive.

Contrary to where I think we're going to go, we go to the penthouse. But when we arrive, Kill tells Hugo to take me upstairs. To put me in the special room while he takes care of something.

"What's the special room?" I ask, my heart racing, too afraid of what he has planned, knowing full well he means what he says. That he's coming into the dark to get me. Thing is, that means I'll have to face it. Look at it head on. I'm not sure I can do that.

"You'll see soon," he says.

"No. I don't want to go."

But he's already got me out of the car.

"I don't suppose you do, but you are. But I'm going in there with you, Cilla."

Panic has me searching the parking garage for an exit, but I know there isn't one. Hugo is behind me and Kill in front. He steps closer, touches my face. "I'll be there with you."

The "special" room is the last one down the hall, three doors past my guest room from the other night. For as luxuriously as the rest of the penthouse is decorated, this room is purposefully bare and cold. Furnishings consist of a double bed without sheets or a pillow, although there's a threadbare blanket lying on the bed. No nightstands, no lamps apart from the overhead. There's an old and damaged side table and rickety chair along the wall that looks like it should have been thrown out several years ago, and above it, a mirror that's cracked in one corner and tarnished. The single window has cheap, broken blinds rather than the lavish curtains of the other rooms. Even the paint on the walls is old. In fact, the only thing that's new in this room is the camera in the corner. He doesn't even try to hide this one. The lens has been trained on me since the moment I set foot in here.

I draw the blanket up and wrap my arms around myself. I'm sitting on the mattress with my back against the wall. There's no headboard. I still have my dress on but it's ripped along the side and I'm barefoot. That's when the dress tore, when Hugo insisted I give him the shoes and I insisted I would not. He won.

An hour must have passed since I've been in here. I thought Kill would be here sooner, but he's probably making me wait it out. Making me anticipate what's coming.

Something has changed between us. It's like we've crossed a bridge that collapsed into the chasm below as we took step after unknowing step on its rickety planks. What's been happening up until this point, I realize now, was child's play. That was the easy part. The part I could survive.

I know he's here before I hear him. It's like I can feel his presence now, I've become so in tune with him. A chill runs up my spine and I shudder. I always seem to have a very visceral reaction to him, even to the thought of him. It's like my body reacts to him outside of the parameters set by my brain.

I hear his voice outside the door. Then Hugo's. I can't tell what they're saying but I can distinguish between the two. A set of footsteps recedes down the hall. Hugo, I assume. When the key slides into the lock, I feel the cold sweat breaking over my forehead. The lock slides back. I push the blanket off and, as the door opens, I force myself to stand. To face what's coming.

Kill stands in the doorway, still wearing his suit jacket. So proper. His gaze slides over me, takes in the torn dress, my bare feet. He steps in and closes the door behind him. The wall at my back is cold against my skin.

He releases me only momentarily from his gaze, hijacking mine again in our reflections in the mirror. He doesn't speak as he slides off his jacket and hangs it across the back of the chair. Purposefully, he takes off one cuff link then the other, sets them on the table, the little sound they make is the only one in the room. He turns to me and my eyes drop to his hands as he begins to roll up one shirt sleeve, then the other. I look at them, at how thick they are, how muscled and powerful. Look at his big hands. Remember how they feel against my skin. How rough he is when he touches me. Takes me.

"I shouldn't have walked away," he says, startling me.

My gaze snaps back to his.

"I shouldn't have left you that way."

"What way?" I ask, backing into the wall even more when he takes a step toward me.

"I know the real truth, Cilla."

I hear him, but I don't want to think about that. All I know is I need to get out of here. Away from him. From his words. From the way he's looking at me.

"I know," he repeats.

"No." I walk around the bed to the window. I can't let him see me now.

"Look at me."

He's close behind me. I shake my head.

When he touches me, I jump, turn to him. I shake my head again, back away, but there's nowhere to go and I'm going to be sick.

"Jones is in bad shape," I say when the wall hits my back. I rub my face, cover it. I can't talk about what he just said. I can't have him look at me. Can't have him see me. Not now.

"I think he's in better shape than you."

I shake my head. "I don't want this."

"I know everything," he says. "All of it."

I double over and hug my stomach. My hair hangs like a curtain between us, shielding me from him.

"Cilla," his voice is low. Dangerous.

I realize I've moved into a squat when he crouches down. As much as I want to crawl into his arms and bury my face in his chest and sob until I drown, when his fingers brush my hair, I slap his hand away. Look at him.

"You don't know anything," I spit. I stand, try to slip past him, but he catches me around the middle, draws me to him, my back to his wall of a chest.

A sob escapes but I swallow it. I can't let this happen. Can't let it start. Because if it does, it won't stop.

"Let me go," I beg. I'm shaking, I'm freezing. I'm too hot. I can't look at him. I don't want to see what I know will be in his eyes because I believe him. He knows. He knows all of it.

He sits on the bed, draws me onto his lap. I keep my face averted as he cradles me.

"It's not your fault," he says.

I break then. That's the moment. It's the kindness. The fucking tenderness in his voice.

"What he did to you. To Jones. What he made you—"

"Stop," my voice is unrecognizable. I'm hiccuping and sobbing and my ears are full of so much noise. So much chaos. "Let me go."

"No."

He keeps his powerful arms around me, hands holding me fast, hugging me to him.

"Just please let me go." His shirt is drenched with my tears and I don't know how there can be so many of them. After so many years, still, all these tears.

"I'm not letting you go, Cilla."

I know he's not. I know. But he has to. I can't do this. I can't. I force my gaze up to his, force myself to harden. "I don't need you," I say. I try to push his arms off. "I don't want you. Not like this."

"No, you want me hard. You want me rough."

I'm confused.

"It's what you need. It's the only way you can bury it. That ends tonight, sweetheart."

He lets me off his lap, stands up, unbuckles his belt.

I shake my head, I don't want to fuck. I turn and try to crawl away, but he catches my ankle.

"It's not a fuck I'm thinking of," he says, as if having read my mind.

When I hear the whoosh of his belt through his loops, I crane my neck back to find him standing over me, doubling the belt, gripping the buckle.

"I think what you need is pain. And maybe then you can

let it out. Let it fucking go. Because holding it, Cilla, it's killing you."

I don't understand and I'm still trying to process when he sits back down, hauls me over his lap so my legs are hanging off one side, and my torso is lying on the bed.

"Forgive me," he says before he rips the dress.

I scream at the sound, at the cool air on the backs of my thighs before the line of fire that is his belt lashes my ass.

Everything stops and I suck in air. But when he strikes again, I fight. I fight hard, trying to get off him, slide off his lap, trying to cover my ass. But he's too strong and he grips my wrists at my low back, drags my panties down my thighs and lashes me with his belt again and again and again.

I can't breathe. I can't keep up. The strokes come hard and fast and I can't fucking breathe.

"It hurts!"

My heart is racing, I'm dripping sweat, my ass and thighs are on fire and still he holds me, his muscular thighs at my belly, his hands trapping my wrists and hugging me to him at once.

"Let it go."

"I can't."

"You can."

I squeeze my eyes shut and fuck, it hurts like hell, and I want him to stop and I want him to hold me forever.

"You can, Cilla. I've got you. I'm right here. You're running like hell but you're in a fucking hamster wheel. Just let it fucking go."

"I can't." I always thought it was Jones who was too broken to be fixed, but maybe I was wrong, because right now, this—whatever the fuck this is—it's breaking me apart. Shattering me into a thousand little pieces.

"You have to."

I hear him and he's still whipping me and all I can do is bury my face in the mattress and sob and sob because I can't hold on anymore. I can't hold this any longer. It owns me. It's been killing me even when I've been thinking that I could control it. That I'd locked it away. It had only been growing. Like a cancer, it had metastasized, infecting all of me with its horror. Because what he did to us, what he made us do, brother and sister, it's sick. It's unnatural. And I can't breathe for the sobbing. I'm drowning. Drowning.

A sound that's more animal than human breaks from my chest and my ass throbs but the belt is gone. Kill lifts me in his arms, sits with his back against the wall and lets me curl into him, lets me bury my face in his chest as much to hide myself as to feel his arms around me.

"Let it out. Let all of it out."

I do. I don't have a choice. It's like a tidal wave, a fucking tsunami of pain and anguish and fear and its coming out of me and I couldn't stop it if I wanted to. And all I can do is cling to him. Cling like he is the only thing keeping me afloat, because right now, he is. If it weren't for him, for his arms around me, I'd drown.

28

KILL

I'm holding her. She's still, finally. I haven't slept but she's been sleeping, knocked out, for hours. She hasn't moved since I stripped off her dress and laid her in my bed. And, I decided, I'm not letting her out of it again. What happened between us tonight, it's bound us. But we were bound before that. We were bound from day one. I knew her darkness. Her damage. It's what drew me. I just didn't realize it would turn into this.

Cilla's curled into me, her face buried against my chest. Her breath is warm against my skin and I think she's peaceful for the first time since I've known her. Maybe for the first time since leaving Callahan's house. His *protection*.

I look down at the top of Cilla's head. Move my hand a little to brush the hair from her face. She doesn't move. Her lips are slightly parted, the last remnant of makeup a shadow on her temple. The skin around her eyes is puffy and pink, and yet she is the most beautiful creature I've ever laid eyes on.

Maybe it's because I've seen her bared. Seen her pain. Slain her dragon.

I don't know how long it is that I watch her but sun is filtering in around the curtains covering the windows when she stirs. She stretches a little, makes a sound almost like a cat purring, feels me beside her, stops. Blinks. Her hand moves to her hip and she sucks in a breath. She'll feel that for a few days, but she needed it. Needed to be forced to release. She was no longer capable of doing it herself.

Jade eyes finally meet mine. I'm curious what I'll find. What she'll say or do. She closes one hand over my shoulder and draws herself up. Her face is an inch from mine, her naked chest pressing against mine.

She doesn't speak, neither does she smile. She only watches me, touches her cheek to the scruff on my face before bringing her mouth to mine. Her lips are tender when she kisses me. I wrap my arms around her waist when she slides closer, then climbs on top of me. She deepens the kiss, and her legs open and my dick is hard for her, but it's not release I seek, and I have a feeling that's the same for her. This is something else. It's a need to seal what happened between us last night. A need to couple. To be joined and fused together, at least for a moment.

"Cilla." I roll her onto her back. Her legs wrap around me, drawing me to her. I kiss her again, cup the back of her head, weave my fingers through her hair. Keeping my eyes on her, I slide into her. This isn't a fucking. It's not hard. It's not me or her taking. It's too tender for that. This is love making, something foreign to me and, I have a feeling, for her.

"Cilla," I say again. I move slowly and she clings to me, our gazes locked on one another, and this feeling, this tenderness, it's strange. I feel everything more acutely than ever before. Feel her body absorb me like I'm a part of her. Like she's a part of me. We're so close, I don't think I've ever been so close to anyone before, not even to her, not even when I was fucking her.

"I love you," she whispers, a tear sliding down the side of her face.

I just stare at her as she lies beneath me, hold her in my arms, possess her.

"I love you," she says again, like she's making sense of it herself. "I love you."

Her eyes glisten, shine like emeralds, and her pink mouth opens and her breathing becomes more shallow as the urge to come dictates my rhythm and it's like I can't slow down, can't drag this out even though it's all I want, to make this last hours. Days. To stay inside her like this forever. But I can't because I need to fill her up, need to feel her contract around me. Need to finish this. And when I do, it's with a human sound, no animal mounting its mate, not fucking with the purpose to impregnate, but making slow love. I come for what feels like an eternity and feel her come and watch her like she watches me, and I know something has changed now. It's not the same between us but I don't have a word to put to this thought, this feeling. I just know it's different, that it will never go back to what it was.

That this, last night and now, this, it's a line of demarcation. Tonight, everything has changed. Every single thing.

"I love you, Cilla."

———

"How did you do it?" Cilla asks once we're showered. She's pulling a sweater over her head and I'm buttoning my shirt.

I know what she's asking but does she really want to

know? Callahan's become crocodile food by now. Crocodile shit.

"I took pound for pound of flesh. Like you wanted."

"How long until he died?"

"Long."

"Not long enough."

"No, probably not, but it's finished now. You have to let it be now."

"Have you let it be? With Ginny?"

The question catches me off guard. I button the last button, look at her, see only curiosity in her eyes.

"I think I did the night I went out there."

"When you came back without your shoes?"

I nod, look off in the distance. "It's the first time I've been back since everything happened. Finding her shoe out there—she always wore ballerina slippers—I didn't expect to find that. I thought they'd cleaned it all up when they took her away. But seeing it, I don't know, in a way, it showed me that it was in the past or something. Like somehow, some way, my own feelings about that night, my rage about what happened to her, they didn't rule me anymore."

Cilla's watching me when I turn to her.

"The one thing that nearly destroyed me was the fact that I'd let her down. That I hadn't protected her like a brother should. Not that she hadn't come to me, but that I'd been too blind to see. Impotence for a man is a cruel sort of death. That helplessness, powerlessness, I felt even when I killed the man responsible, it stayed with me for a long time. Too long. I don't know when it left me, actually, but it has. And that night, I was drunk." I shake my head. "I was so fucking drunk but maybe I needed to be because it felt like she had left her shoe for me to find. Touching it again, putting it between my own, bigger ones, it finished something."

I walk to the window, look outside. Cilla comes up beside me, slips her hand into mine.

"What I did to my uncle, maybe back then I thought I could bring her back by taking his life. I don't know. But she's gone and I think she's at peace. Maybe more so than she could ever be here."

"I'm sorry for what happened to you. To both of you," Cilla says, taking both hands now.

I look down at her. "I'm sorry for what happened to you. To both of you."

She gives me a weak smile and I have a feeling she's also let go of at least some part of the past. That now, she can start to heal.

EPILOGUE 1
CILLA

It's three months to the day that Jones tried to hang himself. I can finally say those words without breaking down, without it breaking me. It's a cold, clear day and snow blankets the fields, outlines the bare branches of the trees. It's so beautiful. White as far as the eye can see. Clean and new and filled with promise.

"I'm freezing my ass off, Cilla."

I smile.

Kill and I are standing outside the entrance of the Dover Recovery Village. He's holding my hand and I can feel him watching me as I stare at the double doors. I take a deep breath in and nod. Kill pushes one of the doors open and we step inside, the gust of wind that sneaks in around us ruffling the papers on the desk in the lobby.

Today will be the first time I see Jones in three months, although I've been talking to him in brief conversations over the phone for a few weeks now. He's doing so well, remarkably well. And so am I. At Kill's urging, I've been talking to someone too, talking about everything.

I underestimated the power of spoken words. I didn't realize they can heal as surely as silence can destroy.

"Good morning, Mr. Black. Ms. Hawking." The same nurse who's always here stands to greet us, the smile on her face easier than I've ever seen it before.

"Good morning. Dr. Moore is expecting us," Kill says.

"Yes, he is." She turns to me and gives me a smile. "And so is your brother."

I'm reassured by this. I don't want to push Jones but it's taken all I have to let things play out like this. I know it was the right thing to do, though. For both of us.

Kill squeezes my hand as we follow the nurse to Dr. Moore's office instead of directly to Jones's room. "Is something wrong?" I ask, confused by this.

"No, the doctor just wanted to talk to you for a few minutes first."

"Okay."

Once we're seated in Dr. Moore's office, he opens a folder and arranges some papers.

"Did he change his mind?" I ask, my heart racing. I've been looking forward to this for more than a week and I don't want him to have changed his mind.

"No," Dr. Moore says, looking up at me as he turns the papers around so Kill and I can read them. I'm surprised at the glimpse I get. They're release papers. "He's looking forward to seeing you."

Kill picks up the pages, shuffles through them.

"I wanted to meet with you to discuss Jones's departure from Dover Recovery Center."

I'm both elated and terrified by this. "Is he ready?"

"I think so. I don't think there's more we can do for him. But I do think he's scared, which is natural."

"He can live with us," Kill says, setting the papers back on the desk.

I'm taken aback by this and shift my gaze to him.

Although I've kept my apartment, I only go back once or twice a week and never sleep there. We spend most of our time at Rockcliffe House these days, but I guess I hadn't thought of it as living together, not until Kill says it that way.

He glances at me, then back at the doctor.

"No, I think he wants to go back to his own apartment and I think it's important for him to do so," Dr. Moore says. "He'll still be coming in twice weekly to meet with me, his suggestion, I thought once a week would suffice."

"That's great," I say. "He must trust you." I push away the thought that my brother trusted his secrets, his pain, to this stranger and not me, but I also know it's easier sometimes to tell a stranger. Easier than having to look someone closer to you in the eye while you give voice to your shame.

"I think he's found a safe place here. You'll see what I mean when you see Jones."

"When—"

"I just wanted you to know about his release. We'll finish out the month here, but after that, he'll be able to resume his life."

"And you're sure he's ready?"

"I am. It won't be without difficulties, the demons are in no way banished, but he is better able to cope."

"He'll need a job," I say, turning to Kill.

"I have an idea," Kill says.

"And my apartment is only a short drive from his," I say, unsure where this leaves us.

"So is the penthouse," Kill says.

"Maybe it's better if I—" I start.

"You'll be at the penthouse," Kill finishes, rising. "I think we're ready."

Dr. Moore clears his throat. "Of course." He steps out into the hallway.

I'm still staring up at Kill. "What was that?" I ask, standing.

He looks at me. "What was what?"

"You'll be at the penthouse," I mimic him.

He raises his eyebrows. "Poor imitation, Cilla. Let's go."

"Wait."

"What?" He seems oddly, mildly irritated.

"Why did you say it like that?"

"You'll be staying with me, Cilla. At the penthouse or Rockcliffe, but it's time you gave up that apartment."

I stare at him, dumbfounded. This changes things. Officially living together changes everything.

For the first time since I've known Kill, there's a single moment of uncertainty in his eyes. Just the briefest flash of it.

"Kill?"

"I'm not doing this here." He hasn't quite met my eyes. "Your brother's waiting."

I smile at his uncharacteristic behavior, put my hands on his face, make him look at me. "Are you asking me to move in with you?"

"You already live with me," he tries.

"Kill?"

"Let's go see your brother," he says, taking my wrists to pull my hands away, walking me out of the office.

Dr. Moore is waiting for us outside. We walk toward Jones's old room where he's been moved back to, and my heart is racing. I don't know what to expect. But when we get there and he pushes the door open after a brief knock and I see my brother for the first time in too long, a wide smile spreads across my face as tears slide down my cheeks.

"Jones!"

He smiles back and it's just as big as mine. When I run to him, he opens his arms and for the first time in more than eight years, we hug. We actually hug.

Kill and Dr. Moore leave us alone at some point, and after a long time, Jones and I sit at the window of his room again, like that last time, except this time, we're holding hands and smiling and not looking at the beautiful scene out the window but each other. And for the first time in too long, I see a spark in Jones's eyes that I remember from home. Our real home with our parents.

"Stop with the tears already, Cilla." He wipes my face.

"They're happy tears."

"I don't care. We've both cried enough for two lifetimes."

"You look really great, Jones. Better than in a long time." He's put on weight again and his color is alive. It's like he's alive again.

"I feel better than I have in a long time. We should have done this sooner, huh?"

"I'm glad we're doing it now."

"You were holding hands with him when you came in."

I smile. "He saved my life. Both of our lives."

"I told you so," he teases. "He's in love with you."

I feel myself blush. "You were right. And you were wrong. He is a beast. But he's also my dark knight. I love him."

EPILOGUE 2

KILL

Summer

Cilla's a pain in the ass. But I guess I knew that going in.

Jones is back at his apartment and thriving. He still goes to see Dr. Moore weekly, although it's down to once a week rather than two now. That's progress. I also got him a job with someone I know working construction. Figured a guy like Jones needs the physical work. It keeps the mind healthy and it exhausts him so he can't get himself into trouble.

Cilla is living with me although she refuses to give up her apartment. I don't know what she's waiting for but it's a waste of money to pay rent on a place you don't use. And, if I'm honest, I don't like the fact that she has it. That she has a place to go that doesn't include me. She's writing again too, but it's a book she's working on now. A children's book.

I park the car at Rockcliffe House and climb out. I see through the sliding glass door that she's out back by the pool. Stripping off my suit jacket, I head toward the back.

She doesn't see me. She's floating on her back in the center of the pool, eyes closed, arms and legs stretched so she's the shape of a star. Her dark hair is fanned out and she looks so peaceful, so relaxed. I smile at the sight of her like this. Mine. All mine.

She opens her eyes a moment later and when she sees me, she smiles, submerges, swims to the edge of the pool.

"You're going to get tan lines," I say, grabbing her towel as she climbs out of the pool.

I hold the towel out to her as she approaches, a wicked look in her eyes. "You'd like me to swim naked, wouldn't you?" she says, ignoring the towel and wrapping her dripping wet body around mine.

"This is an expensive suit," I say, holding her to me. I close my eyes and kiss her, savoring the cool, wet slickness of her mouth, tasting chlorine and her.

"Then you shouldn't be wearing it," she whispers.

"You'd like that, wouldn't you?" I tease with a wink.

I release her, and she picks up the towel, pats herself dry before sitting on the edge of a chair. She's wearing a tiny little yellow bikini. Her little tits press against it, the nipples hard even though it's warm out. I sit down beside her and we look out into the woods.

"How's Jones?" she asks. I went to the construction site to see him today.

"He looks good. Mentioned a date tonight."

"A date?" she turns to me, eyebrows high. "He didn't say a word to me."

"Because you'll nag him."

"I wouldn't."

"You would." I wrap my arm around her shoulders and draw her to me. "Your lease is up in another month," I say.

"You and my lease. It's my apartment, so what's it to you?"

"You spend all your time here. What's the point of keeping it?"

"I don't know. If you piss me off, I can go there?"

"I've pissed you off plenty and you haven't left yet. What are you waiting for?"

She shrugs a shoulder, her face getting serious. "I like what we have," she says, shifting her gaze to me. "I don't want it to change."

"You're scared."

She bites the inside of her cheek and looks back out into the woods.

"If anything changes, it's going to be for the better," I say.

Her smile is non-committal. "I don't want to mess it up. Jinx it. Things are really good right now. I can't really afford to lose that."

"You're not going to. We're not going to. Cilla?"

She's still looking away.

"Cilla, look at me."

She does.

"I'm not going anywhere and you're not going to lose anything. But I have to tell you one thing...it's not enough for me anymore."

I know she doesn't understand when a flash of anxiety darkens her eyes. I reach into my pocket, retrieve the box, hold it out to her.

She looks at it, looks at me, then at it again. Her eyes are filling with tears.

I smile, lift the lid.

Her mouth falls open and she's so quiet, quieter than she's ever been.

She raises a hand tentatively, draws it back, then glances at me once before touching it with the tip of her finger.

"If I'd known all it took to dumbfound you was a ring, I'd have bought you a dozen by now."

She chuckles, but it's a nervous one.

I draw the ring out of the box and take her hand, make her look at me.

"I love you Cilla and I want more. I told you once I wanted everything. This is part of that. I want you to take my name and I want to put babies in your belly and I want to spend the rest of my life with you. Marry me, Cilla."

A tear slides down her cheek. "You can't even ask that, can you?" she says as I slide the ring on her finger. It's a perfect fit.

"I don't want to give you a chance to say no."

She drags her eyes from the ring to me. "I wouldn't. I love you and can't imagine my life without you."

Taking her in my arms, I kiss her, things feeling different already, more complete. I think she feels it too.

"The lengths you'll go to to get your way," she teases when we break the kiss. "I'll call the landlord tomorrow."

"I'm glad that worked then. Now," I stand, draw her to her feet. "Let's go start on those babies."

"Just how many babies are we talking here?" she asks as I lead her into the house and lift her in my arms to carry her up the stairs.

"Lots and lots and lots." I kiss her.

The End

SAMPLE FROM GIOVANNI
A DARK MAFIA ROMANCE

Silk tickles my skin, and it takes me a moment to realize it's the blanket sliding off me. I reach for it, still half-asleep, but when I hear a "Tsk-tsk," my body goes rigid and my eyelids fly open. In the light coming through the sheer window curtains, I see the outline of a man. He's huge and standing at the foot of my bed. I know it's him. I recognize his voice, his build. His aftershave.

"You left before coffee."

I sit up, or try to, but he grabs my ankle and tugs on it and stops me.

I want to cover myself, but the blanket is out of reach, so I lie there, naked. Giovanni smiles and his gaze slowly travels over me.

"Were you expecting me, or do you always sleep naked?"

I kick the leg he's got, but when I do, he tugs me down the bed. Turning me slightly, he slaps my ass hard.

"Ow!" He's not smiling when I look back at him, my hand covering the spot he just hit.

"You deserve more than that."

I realize he's not wearing his suit jacket anymore but has

his shirt sleeves rolled halfway up his powerful forearms. I wonder how long he's been here watching me. There's a dusting of dark hair on his arms, and the only jewelry he's wearing is a heavy, expensive watch.

"What are you doing here?"

"Oh, come on, don't pretend to be surprised. You knew I'd come."

He lets me go, and I scramble back up the bed, sit up on my knees, and grab the pillow to cover myself. Giovanni walks patiently around the bed, and as he does, I watch his movements. He switches on the light. I see he's grinning. Moving much faster than I expect, he grabs the pillow from me and tosses it across the room.

"What are you doing?"

"I didn't get to have dessert," he says, placing one knee on the bed, catching me as I try to scramble off, tugging me into his chest. "Now lie down and spread those beautiful legs, so I can get my dessert."

"You're a freak!" I scream, shoving at his chest, but he only laughs it off and tosses me on my back onto the bed like I weigh nothing. I flip over onto my belly to get away, but he easily catches me by the ankle and tugs me flat and this time, presses a knee to my back. I know I fucked up because he stops. I hear him suck in a breath—or maybe that was me—because I know what he's looking at.

It takes me a minute to turn my head to look over my shoulder and see his eyes, see the serious expression there as he eyes my back, the ugly crisscrossing of lines.

"Get off me."

He drags his gaze to mine. "No," he says, as he keeps me in place with his knee on my back. He just studies me for a long time. Not touching, not moving, Just taking in every inch of my back. And I feel myself shrinking. Feel his power over me growing.

I make a sound, wriggle beneath him, but he easily keeps me pinned and ignores me as he trails his fingers along the thin silvery lines that mark me where the skin broke, where my back was opened, and I feel my face burning because it's private, this thing, it's more private than any part of me. And it shows my weakness. And I don't want him to see it. I don't want him to know it's there at all and that I fucked up.

But then he meets my gaze again, and that grin is back, although forced, I think, at least at first, until it isn't, and somehow, the wickedness of it is a relief.

"You're going to have to tell me that story sometime," he says, then flips me back over and slips off the bed to kneel on the floor, pulling me toward him, spreading my legs, his thick arms beneath my knees, hands gripping my thighs as he roughly brings me to his face.

"What are you—"

I gasp, my hands fisting the sheets as his mouth closes around my pussy and his hot, wet tongue licks me, tastes me, draws back to look at me, then meets my eyes and takes my swollen clit into his mouth and sucks and that sound, those sighs, that moaning, it's coming from me.

He grins, and I close my eyes. Giovanni pulls me tighter to him, devouring me, the scruff on his jaw a rough contrast to the softness of his lips, his tongue, and it feels so good. Too fucking good.

My eyes fly open, and I try to pull myself free, but he tightens his grip.

Fuck, I'm going to come, and he knows it. He can hear it, hear my whimpers, my moans, and when he next takes my clit between his lips and sucks, I do. I cry out, and it takes me moments to come. Fuck, I come so hard I'm bucking against his face, and I hate him and I'm lost and it feels so fucking good that I can't do anything but feel, feel it, feel him, let myself go. Let myself come.

When I open my eyes again, he's releasing me, rising to stand. His eyes, so dark now, are locked on mine. He wipes the back of his hand across his mouth and he's looming over me, and I just lie there, limp. Hollowed out, like he carved out a piece of me.

Planting his hands on either side of me, he leans over and brings his face to mine, inhaling, almost like an animal, like a predator scenting his prey. I swallow, and when he touches his lips to mine, I open for him. But he doesn't kiss me, and he doesn't close his eyes. Instead, he takes my lower lip between his teeth and bites, not hard, not hard enough to break skin.

I feel him against me, his hardness at my sex, and I want him again. I want him inside me. I want to come with him inside me.

And I know from the look on his face when he pulls back that he knows it too.

"Your pussy's greedy, Emilia."

He straightens. My legs are half hanging off the bed, and he's standing between them.

I look at him, confused.

"You don't get to come twice, though. Not after how you behaved tonight." He slaps my hip before he turns and heads toward the door, but stops just before he gets there, and I sit up.

He retraces his steps and, reaching into his pocket, he takes out a stack of bills. He sets them on the nightstand, then reaches for me and grips my jaw, his fingers digging into me as he tilts my face upward.

He's firm when he speaks. Like he's just remembered his annoyance with me. "You don't pay for dinner when I take you out. You eat, and you say thank-you. And you definitely don't walk out. Understand?"

"And then what? I spread my legs?" My heart is racing. I shouldn't challenge this man. I know better.

But he's ready for my comment. I think he likes it from the narrowing of his eyes, the grin on his face.

"That's ideal. Although like I said at dinner, I didn't expect to sleep with you. Dinner wasn't about me buying your pussy. Because that'd make you a whore, wouldn't it? And I don't think you're a whore, are you, Emilia?"

Before I can answer, he releases me. I'm not even up on my useless, shaky legs before he's gone. Out of the bedroom and out of the apartment. I hear the door open and close. Hear the lock turn.

The bastard has a key.

Buy Now!

THANK YOU

Thanks for reading *Killian: a Dark Mafia Romance.* I hope you enjoyed Kill and Cilla's story. If you'd consider leaving a review at the store where you purchased this book, I would be so very grateful.

Want to be the first to hear about sales and new releases? You can sign up for my Newsletter here!

Like my FB Author Page to keep updated on news and giveaways!

I have a FB Fan Group where I share exclusive teasers and interact with readers. It's called The Knight Spot. If you'd like to join, click here!

ALSO BY NATASHA KNIGHT

Collateral Damage Duet

Collateral: an Arranged Marriage Mafia Romance
Damage: an Arranged Marriage Mafia Romance

Dark Legacy Trilogy

Taken (Dark Legacy, Book 1)
Torn (Dark Legacy, Book 2)
Twisted (Dark Legacy, Book 3)

Ties that Bind Duet

Mine

His

MacLeod Brothers

Devil's Bargain

Benedetti Mafia World

Salvatore: a Dark Mafia Romance
Dominic: a Dark Mafia Romance
Sergio: a Dark Mafia Romance
The Benedetti Brothers Box Set (Contains Salvatore, Dominic and Sergio)
Killian: a Dark Mafia Romance

Giovanni: a Dark Mafia Romance

The Amado Brothers

Dishonorable

Disgraced

Unhinged

Standalone Dark Romance

Descent

Deviant

Beautiful Liar

Retribution

Theirs To Take

Captive, Mine

Alpha

Given to the Savage

Taken by the Beast

Claimed by the Beast

Captive's Desire

Protective Custody

Amy's Strict Doctor

Taming Emma

Taming Megan

Taming Naia

Reclaiming Sophie

The Firefighter's Girl

Dangerous Defiance

Her Rogue Knight

Taught To Kneel

Tamed: the Roark Brothers Trilogy

ACKNOWLEDGMENTS

Cover Design by Pop Kitty Designs

Cover Photography By Eric Battershell

ABOUT THE AUTHOR

USA Today bestselling author of contemporary romance, Natasha Knight specializes in dark, tortured heroes. Happily-Ever-Afters are guaranteed, but she likes to put her characters through hell to get them there. She's evil like that.

Want more?
www.natasha-knight.com
natasha-knight@outlook.com

Printed in Great Britain
by Amazon